THERE IS A WIDENESS

A NOVEL

Mark William McAllister

RiverOak®

Good News in Fiction

An Imprint of Cook Communications Ministries
COLORADO SPRINGS, COLORADO   PARIS, ONTARIO
KINGSWAY COMMUNICATIONS, LTD., EASTBOURNE, ENGLAND

RiverOak® is an imprint of
Cook Communications Ministries, Colorado Springs, CO 80918
Cook Communications, Paris, Ontario
Kingsway Communications, Eastbourne, England

**Published in association with the literary agency of Hartline
Literary Agency, Attn: Janet Benrey, R3 Queenston Drive,
Pittsburgh, PA 15235.**

First Printing, 2004
Printed in the United States of America
1 2 3 4 5 6 7 8 9 10 Printing/Year 08 07 06 05 04

Cover photo: © Daryl Benson/Masterfile

Library of Congress Cataloging-in-Publication Data

McAllister, Mark William.
  There is a wideness / by Mark William McAllister.
      p. cm.
  ISBN 1-58919-010-6 (pbk.)
  1. Texas, East--Fiction. 2. Explosions--Fiction. 3.
Schools--Fiction. I. Title.
  PS3613.C265T48 2004
  813'.6--dc22

                                              2003020289

For

William Sidney McAllister

(1916-2001)

and

Genevieve Langham McAllister

(1916-2004)

Writing historical fiction is not a solitary endeavor. With pleasure I acknowledge the help and encouragement of:

Austin folks: Wife and helpmate Janie McAllister, Joan Hall, Melissa Gaskill, Alberta Deacon, John Burch and other fellow writers in the Sunday afternoon Novel-in-Progress group, Tom Polk, Laura Delfeld, Susan Hensley and Carey Suehs.

My agent Janet Benrey; my editors Jeff Dunn and Jimmy Peacock; Georgia Hoff of Roy, Utah (Mrs. Hoff is the daughter of the late Lorine Zylks Bright, see below); David King of Ashfield, Mass.; Ben Welmaker and Harold Palmour of Lufkin, Tex.; Mollie Ward of New London, Tex.; Mildred McAllister of Fort Worth, Tex.; Patricia and James Abney of Rosharon, Tex.; Geneva Willard of Henderson, Tex; Mike Palmieri of New Orleans; and Orey Neal of Livingston, Tex..

The following books provided invaluable setting and background information:

New London 1937 by Lorine Zylks Bright, (Wichita Falls, Texas: Eastex Press, 1977)

The Last Boom by Michel T. Halbouty and James A. Clark, (Bryan, Texas: Shearer Publishing, 1984)

Living Lessons from the New London Explosion by R.L. Jackson, (Nashville: Parthenon Press, 1938)

Grand Coulee by Paul Purtzer, (Pullman, Wash.: Washington State University Press, 1994)

A River Lost, by Blaine Harden (New York: W. W. Norton, 1996)

The Making of the Atomic Bomb by Richard Rhodes, (New York: Simon & Schuster, 1986)

On March 18, 1937, a few minutes after 3 PM, two teachers left the New London, Texas primary school and walked south toward the high school building, a couple of hundred yards away, for a scheduled PTA meeting. They were Genevieve Langham, 20, a music teacher and recent Baylor graduate, and Myrtle Braswell, playground teacher. The two were roommates and best friends. Apparently neither was aware that the PTA meeting, normally held in the high school auditorium, had been moved to the gymnasium behind the main building. The fifth grade children were to put on a little show, a dance, and the gymnasium was better suited for that.

The two had walked to within about a hundred feet of the building when Miss Braswell stopped and said, "I forgot my coat."

Miss Langham was mildly irritated. She knew that "Myrt" only wanted the coat for the cigarettes in the front pocket. Nevertheless she stood and waited while her friend went back. A minute or two later the walls of the building in front of her blew outward, and the roof rose up and came back down, and what had been a school became a pile of rubble and mortar dust and young bodies and body parts.

Shaken but unhurt, Genevieve Langham, the regular organist at New London's Methodist Church, played for thirteen consecutive funerals on March 20.

She continued to teach after the explosion, and in 1940 a man came into her life, an oil man, a chemical engineer, recent Iowa State graduate, quiet, steady, dark-haired, handsome. In 1941 Miss Langham married her beau, Bill McAllister.

I was their first child, born in 1944. We lived near New London for a few years after the war, but I have no memory of those times. My memories are of an oil camp northeast of Gladewater, where my father was appointed superintendent of a gasoline plant in 1947. There under the derricks and pine trees I lived out my boyhood, lulled to sleep every night by the rhythmic thumping of gas compressors in the nearby plant. In the third grade, at Gladewater's Broadway Elementary School, I wrote a bit of fiction. The comet went away to circle the sun, but reappeared forty-five years later to beckon me once again.

Mark McAllister

1

Memory leaks out of an old man like fine sand from a burlap bag, and so I must write down Luke Robertson's story before the details sift away and become lost. Just yesterday I tried to recall the name of that fellow at the dam who found Luke's ledge on the canyon wall, and it was a full ten seconds before "Bob Coleman" popped into my head. Power plant engineer. Worried about the river and the salmon. Sure, now I remember. But what about all the other voices and places and events from Luke's story? Can I recall them? Details matter.

I have mixed feelings about this undertaking. At the center of the story is a tragedy, a school explosion that happened ten years ago in 1937. Here in East Texas the memory of that event is raw and unhealed, and some people will say that writing about the tragedy is like tearing at the wound. I worry that those people might be right.

But I believe Luke's story needs a permanence, and writing it down is the only way to achieve that. Luke is not a writer. I am the one to do it, and now is the time, while my health is still good. I'll be seventy-one in January.

Luke's story links with my own. I have lived the past ten years in a fog of fear and uncertainty. I have held a secret, and the fear of someone learning that secret has caused me to live a solitary and careful existence. But now I see a purpose. I have handed my fears, and my secret, to the winds.

His story begins where many stories end, in a graveyard. I first encountered Luke at Pleasant Hill Cemetery, in the heart of the East Texas oil country, at sundown three months ago.

◆ ◆ ◆

The cicadas sang loudly on that breezeless July evening. Their choruses swelled and died away in a gentle cycle, a celebration of nightfall as the sun dipped beneath the derricks and pines under a cloud-free sky.

I had finished my weed cutting earlier, but the peaceful dusk beckoned me to stay a while and enjoy a quiet reverie. I sat against an oak tree at the southern edge of the cemetery, my face toward the fading western light, and began to wonder: Why *do* the cicadas sing in concert? Do they follow a leader? Or is the rise and fall of their songs timed by some compelling inner force?

I was pondering that very question when my side vision caught a movement. I looked to the north and saw a man walk through the cemetery gate and head south. But where did he come from? I would have heard a car pull in at the little chapel across the road.

The man stopped, looked at a headstone, and eased himself to the ground. He just sat there, staring at the marker. A few minutes passed. I decided it was time to leave. The reverie was broken. Sometimes two live men in a cemetery are one too many.

I stood up, stretched, grabbed the scythe and started toward the gate. My path took me about twenty feet behind the fellow at the headstone. My first thought was to keep walking and pay no attention to him. Like me, he might well have wanted to be alone. But then my curiosity rose up and pushed aside my better judgment.

When I neared the man, I cleared my throat and said, "Evenin'."

He jerked his head around and stared. A few seconds went by, and his silence told me I should have kept walking. The cicadas started a new song, and I was grateful for the racket. But then their chorus faded, leaving only silence and the stare of a bearded man.

I decided to say one more thing, and if he just kept staring I would walk away. I said, "You ... Marty's father?"

When he heard that, his body seemed to twitch. He got to his feet and staggered in my direction.

He was about my height—six foot one—and had a similar build, broad-shouldered and a bit on the husky side. There the resemblance ended. His hair was deep black, matted and greasy. A dark, scraggly beard covered his lower face.

His clothes looked like things any sensible man would have taken out and burned. The sweat-soaked khaki shirt and denim pants were frayed and caked with grime and soot.

He stopped about five feet away and raised a bruised and scarred fist. He pointed a finger at me. In a low, mean voice he growled, "Who are you? What are you doing here?"

"I'm the caretaker. I work here."

He cursed me, with words I hadn't heard in a while, and stepped a foot closer. His bloodshot eyes narrowed. "Caretaker. You said, *Marty*. You tell me why you said *Marty*."

"It's her grave. I figured you—"

"Listen, man, that headstone says *Martha Lee Robertson*. It doesn't say *Marty*."

I said, "It's *Marty* on the monument."

He shook his head and spewed a profanity. "What monument?"

"The monument in town, across from the school. You don't know about that?"

He doubled up his fists and glared at me. "That headstone's

thirty feet away. It's almost dark. You couldn't read the name on it, so how come you know it's her grave?"

"I know where all the school graves are, not just hers."

That was the truth, but I knew it wouldn't mean anything to him. He just stared at me. Neither of us said a word.

Finally he turned around, took one last look at the headstone, and headed toward the gate. He went through it and turned east, toward Henderson. I watched until the darkness swallowed him.

I walked over to the headstone and knelt. There was barely enough light for me to see the date of birth etched into the granite: November 9, 1923. So she was thirteen when it happened. Thirteen plus ten is twenty-three. He didn't look old enough to have a twenty-three year old daughter. No, he was in his thirties, I'd guess, early to mid-thirties.

He was gone. I'd never see him again, but could I forget him? No. The desperate, haggard appearance. The exhausted walk. The low, dry, raspy voice.

I went to my truck and drove west toward home, but pulled off the road and stopped. Why did I fear a man who had just walked out of my life?

Did he live around here? Somehow I doubted it. But he knew where to find a particular grave. And if he wasn't walking home, where was he going? Wherever it was, I figured he'd never make it. He looked ready to drop.

I decided to offer him a drink of water. No possible harm in that. I turned around, drove back past the cemetery, and soon found him in my headlights.

I passed him and pulled to the side of the road, then stepped out and stood by the truck bed. "Hey, Mister, you looked real thirsty back there. Here's a tin cooler with some cold water. Come have a drink."

I tilted the cooler to pour water into the lid, then held it out to him. In the red glow of the taillights his face looked darker than before, fierce, like a wild animal's.

He looked at me, then at the water. He took the lid and drank every drop.

"More?" I asked.

He shook his head, handed back the lid, and said, almost in a whisper, "Thanks, old man. Haven't had much water today." Then he said, "Well, goodnight," and walked away.

"Hey, Mister," I said, and he stopped. "I'm just wondering, where are you going?"

"Longview. Gonna get on a freight train and ride it west." He raised his left hand and wiped sweat from his brow. "Doesn't it ever cool off in this blasted country?"

"Longview's thirty miles. How long since you've had anything to eat?"

He sighed and shook his head. "I'm tired of your questions, Mister."

"I live in Turnertown, about seven miles from here," I said. "I've got some leftover stew in the icebox. I can heat it up for us. Come eat a bite with me, and then I'll drive you to Longview."

He shook his head but didn't move. I stepped into the cab, reached over to open the door, and motioned to him. He hesitated, then got in and closed the door. I shifted to first and let out the clutch, and the truck jerked forward with the usual clatter.

The man said, "You got some burnt valves."

◆ ◆ ◆

We sat at my kitchen table, and he gulped down two bowls of beef stew and four slices of buttered bread. Neither of us said a word while we ate. Finally he put down his spoon, stood up, and said, "Thanks for the meal. I'll get out of your way now. You don't have to drive me. I can walk to Longview."

"Yeah, you probably could. You're a young man. You could walk all night. But you're worn out. Stay here and sleep on the couch. I'll drive you to Longview in the morning."

He gazed at the tablecloth for a few seconds. "You're right. I'm too tired to even argue with you. I'll sleep on your floor. Haven't slept on anything soft in weeks. Wouldn't feel right."

"All right. Suit yourself. If you want to take a bath, that'd be fine."

By the time I'd cleared the table and washed and dried the dishes, the fellow had curled up on the floor next to the sofa and gone to sleep. Hadn't even taken off his boots.

I got a clean pair of overalls, a shirt, a pair of boxer shorts, a bar of soap, and a towel, and laid them on the sofa. Then I took a bath and went to bed, but it was a long time before I slept.

Who was he? Said he planned to get on a freight train and ride it west. Is that how he got here? Might explain the filthy clothes. But his accent told me he'd grown up around here.

He must have been here ten years ago. Here when the explosion happened. Here when Marty Robertson died. Then he went away.

And came back. Must have come a long, long way. Why? To visit a girl's grave? Got to be more to it than that.

To me he seemed like a man who needed help. He needed counseling, consoling, words of assurance. A man I once knew could have said such words, but that man had been gone a long time.

The fellow sleeping on my floor had come to the wrong place. I'd drive him to Longview the next day so he could catch his freight train. I'd wish him well.

That was my plan. Then I thought of Widow Daniels in Henderson, the lady waiting for me to start that landscaping job on her yard, the job I'd been putting off because I couldn't lift a railroad tie by myself.

2

I got up at dawn wondering if the man was still around. Part of me hoped he had walked away during the night, but I found him still on the floor, sound asleep.

I made breakfast and ate, then went to the vegetable garden with the hoe to do some weeding. The morning was clear and cool, the sparrows and jays were singing, and pretty soon so was I. When I work outdoors I like to sing. Singing comes easy to me, unlike talking. I sing the songs I've known all my life. Some folks call them hymns, but to me they're the old songs.

Eventually I turned toward the back porch. The fellow stood there, wearing the clothes I had set out. I yelled, "There's eggs and bacon on the stove. I ate already."

He moved his hand in a little wave and went back inside. A few minutes later I felt the need for a cup of coffee.

He sat at the kitchen table shoveling scrambled eggs into his mouth. He looked up and said, without a smile, "Thanks for the clean clothes and the breakfast. If it's all right with you, I'll wash my clothes, and after they dry I'll take you up on that ride to Longview."

His eyes weren't bloodshot anymore, and I could see that they were dark gray, but they seemed lifeless.

I shrugged. "Okay. Washboard, wringer, and soap are on the back porch." I poured my coffee and sat down at the table.

Without looking at me he said, "I took a bath. Wouldn't be right to put on clean clothes the way I smelled."

I nodded and sipped the coffee.

"Besides, I'm gonna have to beg food to get back north. I'm outta money. You can't beg food when you stink."

"How far north you going?"

"Seattle."

He appeared to think, then said, "Yeah, took me three weeks to get here, and all for nothing. Complete waste of time. Now I gotta get back."

While he finished off the eggs it came to me that I didn't know his name, so I put out my hand. "I'm Russell Smith. They call me Russ."

He shook my hand but there was no heart behind it. "Luke," he said, and stood. "Well, Russ, thanks for breakfast. I'll get to washing those clothes now."

It took him a good half-hour to scrub most of the grime off his shirt and pants, rinse them, and put them through the wringer. It's a wonder they didn't fall apart with that scrubbing. He hung them on my clothesline to dry and sat on the back porch while he waited.

Two paths beckoned me. The safe path would be to take the fellow to Longview and say good-bye. I'd have every reason to feel good about what I'd done for him. Saved him from a thirty-mile walk. Gave him two good meals and a night's rest.

The other path had an appeal too. I needed to fulfill my promise to Widow Daniels, and Luke appeared to be a strong man who could help with the job. He might be grateful for the chance. He might work quietly and steadily and give me no problems, but what if he started asking questions?

I waited until the sun had almost dried his clothes, then sat next to him on the porch. "Luke, I heard you say you were out of money."

"Yeah. So what? I can survive without money. Done it before."

"I need a little help. I can pay you."

He turned to me, and behind that beard I could see a scowl. "What do you mean?"

"I made a mistake. I told someone I could do a job that I really can't do alone."

"What job?"

"Lady in Henderson. Has a big house, but it's built on a slope. The rains are washing her yard into the street. Told her I'd take care of it. Build a three-foot wall of railroad ties on three sides of her yard. Level the inside. Plant some shrubs and small trees, and St. Augustine on top. Put in some steps. She was real happy with the idea. Told me there was no rush, but that was a month ago, and we've had rain since then, and every time it rains I know she's wondering why I haven't started."

"Why haven't you?"

"I can't lift a railroad tie by myself. Thirty years ago I could, but now I can't."

He shook his head. "I need to get out of here. I can't help you."

I was satisfied, even relieved, with his answer. Widow Daniels would have to wait a while. "Looks like your stuff's dry," I said. "Change, and we'll head for Longview."

He took his clothes off the line and went inside. A few minutes later we were headed toward the truck, me in front with key in hand, when I heard him say, "Hey, Mister."

I turned. He stopped and said, "Got a question for you."

My stomach tightened. "What?"

"Last night you said, 'I know where all the school graves are.' What did you mean by that?" He looked straight at me and waited.

"I go out there to cut weeds. There's not much to think about when you're cutting weeds, so I decided to memorize the names. Mental exercise. When you get old you need that."

"Why just the school graves?"

My pulse notched upward. Lacking a quick reply, I shrugged.

He stared at me with narrowed eyes. " I changed my mind. I'll help you build that wall. Guess it won't hurt to have some cash when I go north."

My relief vanished like a popped soap bubble, but I managed a smile. "I sure appreciate it. Probably take us three days. Today and tomorrow we haul ties. My truck only holds ten ties, and we need to get about sixty altogether. That means going to Tyler instead of Longview. Hop in."

We stepped into the truck, and I cranked the engine. Luke glanced back at the blue fumes blossoming from the tailpipe. "You got worn rings too. Burnt valves and worn rings. This thing needs work. Hope we make it."

We drove to the Cotton Belt yard in Tyler, loaded the old ties that the railroad didn't want any longer, and drove to Henderson. Did the same thing two more times that day. I don't think either one of us said more than a dozen words during those hours. Of course inside the truck you almost had to shout to be heard over that old engine's roar.

We didn't get home until suppertime, so I heated the last of the stew and cut some green onions to go with it, and we sat down to eat. About halfway into the meal Luke looked up and said, "You're a quiet man, Russ."

"Reckon so."

"I never got woke up by a man singing hymns before."

I smiled and nodded.

"You ever sing anything besides hymns?"

I shook my head.

He took a few more bites and said, "I bet you sing in a church choir. You're a churchgoing man, and you sing in the choir, right?"

I felt sweat building on my brow. "Nope."

His eyebrows went up. "Never have?"

"Not since I was a boy."

"You ought to. You got a fine voice."

"Well, thank you."

We finished the meal in silence. I was tired from all the driving and went to bed around nine, but I woke up sometime after midnight, thirsty, and walked to the kitchen for a drink of water. Luke was on the couch, breathing deeply in a sound sleep. I got my water, then noticed some items, papers, on the kitchen table. I picked them up and realized they were photographs. The few photographs I owned were in a box in the bedroom, so I figured these belonged to Luke. I naturally felt a certain curiosity. I took the photographs to the bedroom, closed the door, and turned on the bedside lamp. There were six pictures in all, and they were worn around the edges, creased, and discolored.

One showed two smiling little girls and a boy on a white horse. The boy, sitting in back, had his arms around both girls. I guessed that the boy was Luke himself about twenty years earlier.

In the next picture a girl, maybe seven or eight years old, sat in a swing on someone's front porch. She wore a light-colored dress with a dark belt, and had on white socks and black shoes with buckles. Short-styled hair, slightly curled, probably medium-brown, judging from the shade of gray in the photo. One hand on the arm of the swing, the other in her lap. Bright, clear eyes, a soft smile.

The third photo showed three people standing next to one of those biplanes with an open cockpit. At the left was a short bald man, and on the right a dark-haired man, mid-twenties. No beard, but it was Luke for sure. He looked pale and appeared to be forcing a thin smile. Between the men was the girl from the swing picture, older, maybe twelve or so. She had goggles on her forehead, and her hair looked like it had been through a tornado. She beamed a radiant, triumphant smile.

The other three photos were head and shoulder shots of the girl, posed school pictures, different years, different ages.

I turned off the light, went to the kitchen, and put the photos where I found them. I went back to bed. I thought about the pictures, and then it came to me: That's his sister. Ten years ago she died. He left, and now he's back. Luke is the girl's brother, so his name is Luke Robertson.

◆ ◆ ◆

We were up at dawn and had a pleasant, quiet breakfast. I didn't mention the photos, which had disappeared from the table. By late morning we had hauled three more truckloads of ties to the lady's yard.

I had a mental picture of how the wall should look, but now that I had a helper I needed to explain the picture to him. Luke picked up on it pretty quick, and we spent the rest of the afternoon digging a trench for the foundation logs and cutting some of the ties in two so we could use an overlapping pattern like a brick wall and come out even on the ends.

No friendly clouds showed up to block the sun, and Widow Daniels' lot had no shade trees, so we had worked up a good sweat by two o'clock. I had just finished one of my songs when I heard, "Hey, Russ."

Luke had tied a crosstie to the tailgate of the truck and held my saw on top of the tie. "It's gonna take me five minutes to cut through this crosstie. That big saw at my daddy's sawmill could've sliced through this thing in two seconds."

I wanted Luke to work in silence. Safe silence. I tried to ignore him, but he didn't seem to expect a reply from me.

When he finished cutting the tie, he wiped his brow. "You said you know all the names, the school graves. But you never knew any of those kids, did you?"

I shook my head.

He said, "Names don't mean much by themselves, do they?"

I ignored him.

"Do the names Avis, Darla, and Annie mean anything to you?"

I mumbled, "Sisters."

"Yeah, buried next to each other. You know that, but that's all you know. You don't know about the music they made. You would have liked it. Avis knew all the hymns. She could play 'em in her sleep. She played at our first church service. She was twelve that year."

He didn't speak for a half-hour or so while he worked with the saw, but when we began to stack the foundation ties he started up again. He told an episode from his boyhood, and there was something odd about the way he told it. His tone and words seemed more like those of the boy in his story, not those of the downtrodden man telling the tale.

As I listened to him I started to wonder about his mental state. Was he becoming a child again, because the pain of the present was too great? Was he crawling back to the safety of his youth, to the ordinary and hope-filled time before the heartbreak? Is this why he came back, to try in some crazy way to relive his childhood?

Eventually I learned why he was doing it, but at first I just listened. I didn't acknowledge anything he said. I didn't look at him when he spoke. I just listened to him talk while we worked in the sun, and heard the story of a boy becoming a man.

3

Luke

Yeah, Russ, Daddy had a sawmill in Overton. On the south side of town, not far from the tracks. I used to walk down there and watch that big steam-powered saw cut the pine logs. I loved that smell of fresh-cut pine mixed with the smoke from the oak logs in the boiler fire.

My mother was a farm woman. Wilma married Daddy in 1910 and moved into the house he'd built. I was born in that white house, a half-mile north of the mill, in 1913. I remember my daddy's big arms, his jet-black hair, and his thick mustache. He liked to teach me about mechanical things. I knew how a car's engine worked before I started first grade.

Most of the other kids had brothers and sisters. I didn't, but it never bothered me. Never even asked my parents about it. I ate three good meals a day, slept in a warm, soft bed, and learned from a smart daddy who came home from his sawmill happy. Woods and train tracks called me to daily adventures. No boy could want more.

That all changed one year, 1920. Daddy didn't come home happy anymore. He didn't say much at dinner or supper. I'd walk down to the mill on the summer days and wouldn't see any activity.

I went to Mom one day while she was folding clothes and asked her why the sawmill didn't have much business. Mom usually talked straight with me.

She said, "The farmers don't have money. Can't afford lumber. They don't get much money for their crops now."

"Why?"

"Nobody knows the whole reason. Some people say it's because the war is over. We helped feed Europe during the war, but now they're back in the fields. They don't need our food and grain."

That confused me. "You mean things are better during a war than after a war?"

She smiled. "No. It's better they're not killing each other. The farmers here, they'll just have to be patient and wait for prices to go back up. And you and I will have to be patient too."

"Will Daddy be patient?"

Her smile faded. "Your father takes his business very seriously. Let's you and me be careful and not remind him about it, all right?"

"Sure."

But I forgot my promise at supper one night. I told Daddy I'd like to work down at the mill when I got older. He pushed back his chair and left the house without a word.

I learned that when the farmers suffer, everyone in a farm town suffers, all the businesses. Everybody seemed uneasy, worried. I spent most of my time alone that summer, wandering the woods.

That next winter was so cold the ponds froze over for days at a time. I thought the bleakness and gray would never end. Then a day came in April when everything seemed right again. The sun felt good on my skin, and a warm breeze from the south brought the sweet smell of the forest. It happened to be a school day though.

At recess a tow-headed kid named Mike came to me and said, "Let's go to the woods." Mike, the class troublemaker. I never had gone along with him before, but I had a need, an urge, to be out of that schoolyard and in the forest. I said okay.

We watched the playground teacher, and when she turned the other way for a second we were ready. We slipped away and headed for the tracks, the branch line between Overton and Henderson. We balanced on the rails and walked east.

A half-mile down the tracks we headed into the woods. Mike took a box of matches from his pocket and said, "Let's make a fire." We piled up a bunch of pine needles and scraped the ground bare in a ring around the pile. He struck a match, and we watched the orange flames grow and the white smoke drift up and to the north.

"Make it bigger," Mike said. We piled on more needles, and the fire crackled like it was alive, happy. The flames leaped up level with our necks. Then Mike did something real dumb. He picked up a dead pine branch about five feet long, covered with brown needles, and threw it on the pile. That stick caught fire right away, and part of it lay outside the ground we'd scraped bare. The wind seemed to pick up, and pretty soon two fires burned, one inside the ring and one outside, and the one outside began to spread. We tried to stomp it out. The thick white smoke burned my nose and throat.

I panicked and screamed, "We got to get help!" I ran toward the tracks, toward town. Mike ran the other direction, deeper into the woods.

In town I ran to Mr. Ross's garage, across from the depot. A few minutes later a dozen men with axes and shovels followed me to the fire. I watched them clear a firebreak, and wished I was as old as the men, and as strong.

The fire burned itself out, leaving an acre or so charred. When I saw things were under control, I tried to ease away, but a man pointed to me and said, "He came to get us. He must have started it."

Then Mr. Grimes, the railroad agent, motioned to me. "Come with me, son." He put his hand on my shoulder and walked me back to town, to the sawmill. He told my daddy what had happened.

I thought my daddy's eyes were going to pop out of his head. "With all the trouble I've got, now you bring me this!" He pointed to a big uncut pine log. "Bend over that."

"Mike lit the fire, Daddy." My words had no effect. He took off his belt and whipped me while the sawmill hands watched. Now, he'd whipped me before, but not with a rage, like that day. I can still remember the loud pops, the sharp stings, one after another.

He finished and told me to go home. I walked outside the mill, crying, and started to run. But I didn't run home. I ran through town, to the north, along dirt roads. I headed into the woods and ran until I couldn't breathe. I fell onto the pine needles face down. I cried for a while, but then my breathing slowed, and I just lay there, my chin on the back of my hands.

I stared at the shadow of a big pine limb a foot in front of me. I could actually watch the edge of the shadow moving slowly toward me. I stayed still and watched the shadow creep closer. Finally it covered my head, then moved on down my back. I must have lain there for a solid hour, not moving, just watching the shadow, first the front side of it, then the back. The forest was so quiet. I felt the pain of my whipping ease away, like the shadow was taking it.

A movement caught my eye—a blue jay, on a pine branch to my left. In the stillness the birds weren't even aware of me. The jay flew from the limb and lit on the trunk of a dead tree to my right, then took off and disappeared.

I stared at the dead tree. It had fallen against a little ridge, and there was a space beneath the bottom of the trunk and the ground next to the ridge. I crawled under the trunk and looked up. The trunk and a big branch made a kind of roof, and I realized with a thrill that a few more logs on top and on the sides would make it a perfect little hideout, a tree cave.

Russ, I forgot all about that whipping. I didn't even care when Daddy almost whipped me again for not going straight home. I went back to that tree the very next Saturday and cut logs with my hatchet and built my hideout. It was my place. No one else knew about it. For the next three summers I went there just about every day. I still explored the woods and followed the creeks and walked the rails, but my castle, my base, was the tree cave. And I never dreamed a day would come when I'd want to share it with someone.

My room was next to my parents' room. Most nights after I went to bed I could hear tones coming through the wall. My mother's light tones went up and down, like a song, a melody. Daddy's tones were deeper, flatter, steadier. The tones gave me comfort, and usually put me to sleep.

But sometimes my folks argued with loud voices, and I could make out the words. One winter night just after my tenth birthday, I woke up and heard my mother say, "You were drunk. You didn't give me time. You're drunk now."

Daddy said, "I can barely feed a family of three, and you do this. Maybe I'll sell the sawmill. Then we can buy milk. Yeah, I'll sell it. Know what Van Horn told me? 'Can't afford to rebuild my barn, Walter. Not getting anything for my peanuts this year.' And that cheapskate, Raines. He said, 'Could I have a little more time to pay you, Walter?' I despise those jackasses that won't pay me what they owe me."

The floor creaked, then a door slammed shut. I heard footsteps on the front porch, then silence. A few minutes later Mom's tones came through the wall. I guess she was talking to herself. Her tones were flat, without melody, like Daddy's.

The next day at school I asked some kids what the word "drunk" meant. One boy told me about something called alcohol. It was made with a "still," whatever that was. Alcohol doesn't taste good, the boy said, but when you drink it, you talk louder.

At breakfast two days later my mother turned to me after Daddy said the prayer. Her mouth formed a smile, but her brown eyes didn't light up like when she was really happy. She said, "We have good news. You're going to have a little sister or brother later this year."

I thought about what she said while Daddy ate and looked at his plate. I asked, "You're going to have a baby, Mom?" and she nodded.

Daddy turned to me and said in a real flat voice, "Your mother is going to need rest and quiet. If you get into any trouble at all, at home or at school, I will use the belt. Do you understand?"

"Yes, sir." I noticed Mom's little smile had gone away.

I walked to school confused that day. I'd always thought a baby was a good thing. Did they argue and frown before *I* was born too?

In the spring Mom found out that Rachel Erwin, who lived one street down from us, was going to have a baby too. Rachel became my mother's first good friend. She was younger than Mom, and shorter, plump but pretty, with a soft face, big blue eyes, and dark brown hair that shone. Mom started to smile and laugh again after she and Rachel became close.

The summer seemed to last forever. I spent most of my time in the woods, trying to imagine a brother or sister. I thought about how I would take my brother to the tree cave. But … a girl? I thought about it and decided that a girl could like the tree cave too.

Fall came, and school days. By October Mom seemed huge. Rachel's extra weight didn't change her appearance much.

One night my dad's hand on my shoulder jerked me from

sleep. He said, "Get dressed, you're going to the Erwins'. The baby's coming."

Rachel put a sheet and blanket on her couch and told me to sleep there. Then she went back to our house while Daddy got the doctor.

I didn't sleep a bit. Awful visions crowded my brain, visions of how the baby would get from inside my mother to outside. I knew the process must be scary because my folks had never said much about it.

Long hours later the room was gray, not black. Still, the visions. Finally a few spots of sunlight danced on the wall, and I heard the chirps of sparrows. Their songs pushed the visions away.

Footsteps on the front porch jarred me. My daddy opened the door and looked at me with tired, red eyes. My heart raced. "Is Mom all right, Daddy?"

"Yes. Come see your sister."

I stood at the door, afraid to go in, but then Mom looked over with a smile, and this time her eyes smiled too. She motioned to me, and I went to the side of the bed. Her head rested on a folded pillow, and her right arm held a little white blanket.

She said, real softly, "Look at what God can do," and opened the blanket. I stared for a long time. Nothing had ever given me a joy like the sight of that pink baby.

Finally I said, "Can I hold her?" Mom nodded. I took the blanket from her arm and lifted it and kissed that baby on the head. The baby made a little noise. I froze. "Is she all right?"

"Yes. I think she liked your kiss. Will you help me take care of her?"

Russ, the thought of taking care of that baby gave me a thrill I can't even describe. "Oh, yes," I said. "I want to take care of her."

I rocked the baby girl a long time, until Mom finally held out her arms.

◆ ◆ ◆

Later that day my dad called me back to the bedroom. Mom said, "Luke, we decided to name our little girl Martha Lee. My grandmother's name was Martha. Do you like that name?"

I nodded. Then she told me to write that name in the open Bible on the table next to her bed. Daddy handed me a fountain pen, and I wrote that name on the line under my own name, and the date, November 9, 1923. I looked up and saw my mother's smile. I looked at that baby sleeping beside her, and for some reason a Sunday school hymn came into my head. You know the one.

All things bright and beautiful,
All creatures great and small,
All things wise and wonderful:
The Lord God made them all.

◆ ◆ ◆

In bed that night I thought about the name Martha. I remembered it from somewhere. School? Church? Finally I made the match. Martha. That smart, pretty tomboy in the school reader. She climbed trees and explored the woods with her friends and her dog. But nobody called her Martha, they called her by her nickname.

Mom didn't like it at first when I started calling the little girl Marty. She told me to stop, but I couldn't. I tried to say Martha, but it just didn't sound right.

For the next month or so, Mom called her Martha, and I called her Marty. Daddy always called her "the baby."

By Christmas Mom had relented. The name written in the Bible was Martha, but the name on our lips, the name that rang through the house, was Marty.

4

***

Russ

The storytelling Luke seemed a very different person from the angry man in the cemetery. Yet his story had such a coherence, a connectedness, that I no longer doubted his mental stability. One thing seemed clear—he had a lot more to tell.

We worked until almost dusk and got the first layer of ties in place, leaving an easy job for us the next day. On the way home I got to thinking about what to cook for supper, but as soon as we got out of the truck I knew that problem was taken care of. The south wind came through the house toward us and carried a familiar scent. Sure enough, we walked into the kitchen to find a bowl of fried chicken on the table, wrapped in tinfoil.

I cut up some cucumbers and tomatoes to go with it, and we ate in pleasant silence. A few minutes into the meal Luke looked at me and said, "You're a quiet man, and I know you like to eat without talking, but I really was expecting you to say something about that bowl of chicken."

"Good, isn't it?"

"Yeah, it's good, but we walked into the house and there was a bowl of chicken on the table. Who put it there?"

Just what I didn't want in the middle of a tasty meal, a question that would lead to more questions.

"A lady from my church brought it."

Luke's eyebrows rose. "Let me guess. Widow lady who's sweet on you, right?"

I shook my head and bit into a drumstick.

"You ever been married?"

I nodded.

"Your wife pass away?"

I nodded.

"When?"

"Nine years ago."

"Yeah, there's a widow lady who likes you, Russ. You're pretty good looking for an old guy. Thick silver hair, tanned face. Not the first time that lady's brought you food, is it? Say, when you thank her for that chicken, thank her for me too."

It looked like the only way to stop Luke's questions was to tell the whole story. "Yes, she's brought food before. But she's a married lady, not a widow. And I won't be thanking her because she doesn't know that I know who she is."

"Huh?"

"Started about six months after I moved here, back in '39. Came home one day to find an apple pie on the table, just where that chicken was today. A very tasty pie. I figured somebody would tell me they'd left it there, but nobody ever did. A month later I found a blackberry cobbler. I asked my two neighbors if they'd seen a car stop that day, and they told me no. Well, there's another way you can get to my house. You can park on the country lane just west of here and come past my vegetable garden. My neighbors wouldn't see a car in that case.

"For several years the food showed up every month or so—pies, cakes, cobblers, chicken. I'd always wash the bowls and leave them out on the table so whoever it was could get their bowls back. Even left a note with a bowl one time, expressing my thanks. The person took the bowl but left the note.

"No one ever acknowledged bringing the food. Finally one day in 1943 I happened to be driving from Arp to Henderson on 64, the road just south of here. I looked down the country lane and could see a car on the roadside just about even with my vegetable garden. I pulled onto a side street, parked, and waited. Pretty soon the car backed out onto the road and headed toward the intersection with 42. I got the make and color of the car. I drove on to my house and found a peach cobbler on the table. The next Sunday after church I saw a woman get into that same car. I knew her name, but had never spoken to her.

"Well, who is it?"

I shook my head. "Can't tell you. The lady wants it to be a secret. I have to respect that. Now listen, this is the most I've talked in a long time. My throat's starting to get sore. Could we be quiet for the rest of the night?"

Luke complied with my wishes, and in the days that followed he was generally quiet after we got home at night. Only when he was out under the sun, working with his hands, did the words of his story come forth.

5

Luke

Rachel gave birth two weeks after my mother, and named her little girl Marie. That name lasted about a year and a half. The mothers lived only a block apart, so the two girls spent a lot of time together, and when Marty started to talk, one of the first words she tried to say was the name of her little pal. But she shortened it to "Rie." Cute, we thought, so the moms and I started using that name, too. "Marie" faded away, like "Martha."

Rie had dark brown hair and blue eyes. Somehow you could tell even back then that she would be a beautiful woman, and that's how it turned out. Marty's hair was a lighter brown, and her eyes were just about the same color, like Mom's. She learned to talk earlier than Rie. Oh, did she like to talk, and learn new words. I'd come home from school, and she'd be at the screen door waiting for me, yelling my name as I walked up the drive to the front porch. She'd talk to me, using new words she'd learned that day, so proud of herself. Rie was quieter, from the beginning, but she had a laugh that could make anything seem funny. Mom and Rachel said that Rie learned to laugh so she would have more time to think of something to say after Marty talked. Rie was a little more of a thinker, but Marty, she was the talker.

I spent many hours playing with those two girls, but on school days, between the time school let out and suppertime, it was usually just Marty and me. Some days we'd go down to the creek about a half-mile from the house. Marty loved to explore on her own, throwing rocks in the water, looking for spiders and lizards, climbing on the creek bank. I'd stay real close to her, of course. She'd turn and smile at me every now and then, and those brown eyes glowed with joy of life.

One afternoon we came back from the creek to find Daddy home early. He sat on the sofa, his head low, his elbows on his knees. He didn't look up when we came in, and Mom motioned me into the kitchen.

"He had to let go another hand at the mill," she whispered. "Now there's only one man besides him, and he'll have to help that man with the hauling and cutting and stacking. It will be hard. He's not a young man."

An idea popped into my head. "I'll help him. I'll go after school."

Mom turned away and put her hand to her face. Then she leaned down with wet eyes and hugged me. "You're a sweet boy. Maybe in a few years you can help him."

Daddy didn't say a word at supper, and he didn't even look at Marty, who talked up a storm. How could a man not be happy with a sweet little girl like Marty in the house?

August of that year, 1925, brought a miserable, sapping heat. I decided to build a wagon to pull Marty and Rie in, and was in the garage one afternoon cutting lumber when a car pulled into the dirt driveway. Rachel and her husband Tom got out, and a man I knew as the doctor left the driver's seat. All three faces were grim and tight. They glanced at me, but didn't wave or speak. They went to the front porch and knocked, and my mother let them in.

A strange dread came over me, and my heart beat faster. But I was curious too. I walked toward the house. I heard subdued voices and moans. I stopped.

A minute later Tom came to where I stood, put his hand on my shoulder, and said, "Come in the house." On the way to the porch he said, "Your father is dead. He had a heart attack at the sawmill."

I wanted to run, to the railroad tracks, to my tree cave, any-where. But what about Marty? I forced myself up the steps and through the door. Mom lay on the sofa, her pale face wet with tears. I went to her, and she held me and said my name over and over. I felt like I needed to take care of her and Marty, but I didn't know how. I cried along with her.

◆ ◆ ◆

The church filled up for the funeral. The preacher talked about how Daddy had come from Mississippi twenty-four years earlier and discovered a land he loved. He talked about how Daddy had found an East Texas girl to marry, and how they'd brought new life into the world.

But he talked too long. I felt an anger toward him. That church was like an oven.

◆ ◆ ◆

My mother showed great courage that fall and winter. She tried to hide her worries about money. She hardly ever cried in our pres-ence. But I could hear her sobs, her sad tones, through the wall at night.

I needed to do something. One day I went down to the garage and asked Mr. Ross if I could work there after school, cleaning, doing odd jobs, whatever.

Mr. Ross had been a good friend of Daddy's, but he shook his head and said, "Dewey doesn't like kids." Dewey was the mechanic, a thick-necked, thick-armed, tobacco-chewing bachelor with curly brown hair.

"Sir, I helped my dad work on his car. I helped him replace the brake shoes, and clean the cylinder heads, and change the oil. I can help Dewey like I helped Daddy."

Mr. Ross glanced at Dewey's legs, sticking out from beneath a car, then turned back to me. "We'll try it. Three days a week. Ten cents a day. Dewey'll decide whether you can stay or not."

The first thing Dewey said to me was, "Stay out of the way." I did that at first, while I swept and cleaned tools, but I watched Dewey work. I started bringing him the tools and rags and solvents as he needed them. Dewey got to like me after a few weeks, and even let me help him on some jobs. I learned more about cars, a lot more than my dad had taught me.

After about two months Mr. Ross raised my pay to fifteen cents a day. I gave the money to Mom.

Springtime brought new hope. Mom found a buyer for the sawmill equipment, the owner of another sawmill up on the T&P main line near Longview. We were sad to see them haul all that equipment away, but the money my mother got kept us going.

6

Russ

The verandah of Mrs. Daniels's white house held some wicker chairs, and after we put the last railroad tie in place around four o'clock that afternoon, Luke and I sat on those chairs to rest.

Another crossroads. The retaining wall was complete. I could finish the rest of the job myself. Pay Luke off, drive him to Longview, send him on his way.

But it felt good to have a helper. A man works better and feels better when he has a helper. I'd tried to hire helpers in the past, when I had more business than I could handle. One boy worked out okay, but the oil field pays more, and that's where he ended up.

Luke was a strong man and a steady worker. He was telling me a story, and I did have a vague worry about his motivation for doing that, but his curiosity about me seemed to have waned.

I was just about ready to speak up when Luke said, "You're gonna need some help finishing this job, aren't you? Quite a few truckloads of dirt to fill in behind that wall, then the topsoil, then the St. Augustine, the shrubs, the trees. Us working together, about three days."

Why did his words bother me? I had already decided to ask him to stay.

I took a deep breath. "All right, Luke. Thanks for the offer. We'll start hauling the dirt day after tomorrow."

"Why not tomorrow?"

"Tomorrow's Sunday. We don't work on Sunday."

He frowned, shook his head, and muttered something under his breath.

◆ ◆ ◆

For supper I fixed fried potato slices, corn on the cob, green onions, and tomatoes to go with the leftover chicken. Just as we started to eat Luke said, "Russ, you got any grandkids?"

"Six."

"Where are they?"

"Dallas, all of 'em."

"You got a son or daughter or both?"

"Two sons, one daughter, all in Dallas."

A pause for a swallow of tea, then, "Have you always lived out here?"

"No."

"Well, where did you live before?"

"Different places. Moved around."

"Guess I'm a little curious about why an old fellow would live out here in this little community. Why don't you live in Dallas, near your sons and daughter?"

I began to regret my earlier decision. "I'm a country fellow. I don't like big cities."

"You always done landscaping and gardening?"

I paused. I couldn't lie to him. "No."

Sure enough, his next question was, "What did you do before?"

I took a bite of chicken and chewed it slowly. "I worked in a hospital, but I don't want to talk about that right now."

Luke shrugged and finished his meal in silence. I didn't look directly at him, but I could feel his eyes on me. Was my answer sufficient to keep him from probing further? For the time being, perhaps. Three more days and nights, then he'd be gone. I told myself not to worry.

◆ ◆ ◆

The next morning after breakfast I put on my gray suit and my dress shoes and walked to the back porch where Luke sat staring toward the garden.

"Luke, I've got a second suit that you'd fit into. Want to come to church with me?"

He grunted. "I don't go to church. Learned all I wanted to know about God ten years ago."

When I didn't reply he said, "Used to go. Marty did too. Sunday school and church both. She hardly ever missed. You know, I bet a lot of those kids in that cemetery went to church every Sunday. You ever think about that when you're cutting weeds out there?"

The man from my past would have known what to say, and would have said it. And more. But I couldn't think of anything, so I went to my truck and drove on to the church.

On a humid Monday morning we began to haul the dirt needed to fill in behind the crossties.

7

Luke

Overton finally got electricity in 1929, and Tom Erwin was one of the first in town to get his house wired for lights. Well, Marty ran in one afternoon and asked the question Mom had been expecting. "Can we get 'lectric lights like Rie has?"

Mom told her that we didn't have enough money. We'd have to wait.

Mom and I took turns reading to Marty in bed before she went to sleep, and that night was my turn. After I read to her and kissed her goodnight, I started to turn out the lamp when she said, "Luke, do you know anything about 'lectricity?"

"Yeah, a little bit."

"Can you fix our house so we can have 'lectric lights?"

I started to explain why not, but there was such a look of hope and love on her face that I couldn't do it. I told her I'd look into it. She gave me a wide smile and a big hug. I went to bed thinking, If electricity is good enough for the Erwins, it's good enough for my family.

Tom let me inspect the wiring in his house and told me the man had charged thirty-five dollars for the work. I knew we couldn't afford that. Mom's income from the sawmill sale was just enough for our food and clothes and gasoline. I asked around and added up the costs of the wire, fuse boxes, fuses, switches, junction boxes, outlets, sockets. On top of that, the power company would charge for dropping a line to the house. I decided that we could afford it if I did the inside wiring. I went to Mom.

We sat at the kitchen table, and I showed her a sketch of the house and the outlet locations.

"What about the monthly bill, son? You know we're barely getting by."

"I figure the bill won't be more than about four dollars if we turn off lights when we leave the rooms. My eight dollars a month from working Saturdays at the garage will easily cover that."

She stared at the sketch. "I heard that if the wiring's not done right it can cause a fire."

"Do you think I would do anything that would put you and Sis in danger? I know how to isolate the wires, Mom."

She put both hands to her forehead. "Don't make me decide this, Luke."

Something changed between us right at that moment. I touched her arm and said, "I'm going to do it, Mom. I don't like the idea of Rie and Rachel having lights, and you and Marty not having them. I'm going to wire the house."

She let out a long breath, and nodded. "I'm tired. I need to lay down."

"Are you all right, Mom? You've been very tired lately. I'm worried."

"I'm fine."

When I finished the wiring, we had a little party. The four of us—Rie was there, of course—sat around the kitchen table after dark with all the kerosene lamps in the house turned down. Then I reached up and turned the switch on the base of the bulb, and a bright light filled the kitchen. The girls and Mom clapped and cheered, and Mom told me she was so proud of me and wished Daddy could be there to see it.

◆ ◆ ◆

That year I started ninth grade. Early in September, Tom Erwin took me aside and told me I ought to try out for the football team. I did, and found I liked football. I played tackle. I started the second game of the season, the only ninth-grader to start. Marty and Rie and Mom loved to come to the games and cheer me on.

For the 1930 season the players chose me as team co-captain. In the third game that year we played Henderson, our big rival. Near the end of the first half, I looked over at my personal cheering squad and saw Rie and Marty but not Mom. Vicky Orr sat next to Rie and Marty. Vicky, one grade below me, was a cute brunette who made straight As. I'd never talked to her much, but she usually sat next to Mom and the girls at the football games.

The second half was a roller coaster. We got ahead, then they got ahead. I played almost every down. We finally won, and the crowd went wild.

I walked home after the game and noticed a car in our driveway. I recognized the car, and my heart pounded. It was the doctor's car that had pulled into our drive five years earlier when they came to tell us that Daddy had died. I ran to the porch and jerked open the screen door.

Rachel and Vicky rose to greet me. Sis was in the chair, wiping away tears. Rachel said, "She's all right, Luke. The doctor's with her. She had trouble breathing."

"What? When?"

Vicky said, "During the game she told Marty she didn't feel good and needed to go home. I told her I'd walk the girls home after the game. When Marty and I got here, Marty found your mom on the bed in a sweat, having trouble breathing. I ran to get Mrs. Erwin and then the doctor."

"I'm scared," Sis cried, so I bent down and put my arms around her.

I held her and rocked her. I happened to glance at Vicky. She was staring at me, eyes wide, eyebrows up.

The doctor came out and said Mom was breathing better, but she'd need rest and would have to have some tests done at the hospital in Tyler on Monday. Rachel said she'd bring us supper, then she and the doctor left. Vicky left a few minutes later, after telling us three times to let her know if she could do anything for us.

In early October, Mr. Joiner's well, the Daisy Bradford #3, came in a gusher.

Columbus Joiner was an old wildcatter. He was about the age you are now, Russ, when that well came in. He lived in Dallas but spent a lot of time in Overton. He'd been building up leases for about five years before he managed to get enough money to drill. He did drill a well, out on Mrs. Bradford's farm between Overton and Henderson, but the drill pipe got stuck, and they had to abandon it. He drilled a second well and had to abandon it too. By then he was considered a joke around here. Nobody believed he'd ever find oil. Oil companies had drilled in Rusk County before, and all the wells were dry holes.

He kept at it. Got a new driller and started a third well. Took him a year and a half, but he finally hit the Woodbine sand and brought in the well.

That gusher caused a lot of excitement in the county, but I didn't pay it much attention. I knew that Mom was not recovering from her illness, and bills for doctors and medicines kept coming in.

I decided to quit school and look for a job during the Christmas holidays. Of course I'd have loved to work at Mr. Ross's garage, but I knew he couldn't support two full-time mechanics.

I had heard about the "Depression" for the past year, but things hadn't seemed much different to me. I figured the Depression was pretty much a big-city affair. But I learned otherwise when I went out to look for work. I went to Tyler, Henderson, Kilgore. Asked at all kinds of businesses. No jobs.

Rachel fixed a nice Christmas dinner for our two families. After all I'd been through the previous week, it was good to have a tasty meal and hear Marty's happy chatter and Rie's laughter. Mom even seemed a little better that day. She coughed less, and had more appetite than usual. Still, the ugly word "consumption" hung over her like a dark cloud.

◆ ◆ ◆

Longview was just about my last hope. On a cold morning two days after Christmas I headed in that direction. A few miles beyond Kilgore I saw a truck loaded with pipe at the side of the rode, facing south. The driver stood by the raised hood, hands on his hips. I pulled over, parked, and approached the driver, a short fellow with curly red hair.

"Trouble, Mister?"

"Son, thanks for stopping. Load shifted, so I stopped to tighten it. Now the engine won't crank. Guess the battery's bad."

"Mind if I take a look?"

"Go ahead."

I turned on the truck headlights, and they worked fine. I went back to my car for a cable and hooked it between the truck's battery and the solenoid terminal. No spark.

"Looks like an open solenoid, Mister. I work in a garage. We see this sometimes."

The man rubbed his hand through his hair. "Oh, boy. Now I've gotta find a mechanic. What a day."

I saw an electric winch in front of the truck's radiator, and the truck sat on a bit of a downhill slope. If the winch could move the truck, I could probably get the thing started. I told the driver my idea, and he said to go ahead and try it.

I reeled off the cable and tied it to a pine tree near the edge of the road. I got in the cab and turned on the ignition, pushed in the clutch, and shifted to first. The driver started the winch, and the cable tightened. Sure enough, the truck started to move forward, so I eased out the clutch, and that motor caught and rumbled to life. I shifted to neutral, set the brake and hopped out of the cab.

The driver said, "You're good, son. Real good. How much I owe you?"

"Nothing. But Mister, I'm looking for work. My dad died, and my mother's sick, and I got a little sister. You know anywhere I could find work?"

He thought for a minute. "Get in your car and follow me. I'm not the boss where we're going, but there's a chance Mr. Cain can use another hand."

◆ ◆ ◆

I followed that truck through Kilgore and onto some country lanes. Finally we came to a clearing, and I looked out at the first oil derrick I'd ever seen.

Made of wood, it stood taller than the highest pines in the nearby forest. At the base was a wooden platform about forty feet on a side. At the back of the platform were big steel drums wound with cables. I saw big drive chains, gears, and steam pipes. A pulley block hung suspended from the top of the derrick, and big metal arms dangled from the block. A bunch of long pipes stood stacked on one side of the derrick, and other pipes lay on a rack next to the platform.

The truck driver came back to my car and told me to wait, that he'd go talk to the driller. I got out and watched what was happening on the rig floor. It didn't take long for me to figure out what the men were doing with the metal arms. They were pulling pipes off the stand, attaching them to pipe that was already in the hole, and using the arms to lower the whole string of pipes.

I crawled up on the truck to get a better view. I was fascinated. Those guys on the platform moved those big, heavy pipes around like they were made of cardboard.

The driver came back with another man, so I jumped down from the truck. The man introduced himself as Bill Cain and thanked me for my help. He asked me some questions, about where I'd worked before, that sort of thing. Finally he said that if I wanted a job I could be a roustabout, but that I had to work for no pay that day. If he liked the way I worked, I could come back tomorrow and start earning four dollars a day. We shook hands.

My first task was to help the driver and another roustabout unload the pipe from the truck onto the rack. While we waited for the other roustabout, the driver told me about the driller.

"They call him Checkbook Cain, 'cause he once fired every roughneck on a job at the Wortham field and came around to hand them their last checks. He's tough, but he'll treat you right if you do good work."

"Then we'll get along fine."

"You got lots of confidence for a young man. That's good. You'll need that if you're gonna work in an oil field."

"What oil field?"

"Son, they took a core on this well two weeks ago and brought up oil sand. This well is thirteen miles north of Joiner's. When they bring in this well, and that could be tomorrow, people are gonna know there's a field at least thirteen miles long. That's a big field.

This place is gonna explode. They'll be drilling all over. You'll have all the work you want, boy."

Well, it turned out that driver knew what he was talking about. Except he was wrong about the size of the field.

I worked hard the rest of the day, digging holes for a storage tank's concrete supports and cutting firewood for the boilers. I came home starved. Luckily Mom and Sis had saved me some roast beef and potatoes from their meal.

Marty was upset that I was quitting school to take a job, but Mom didn't argue. When I told her I'd have to work the next day, a Sunday, she said, "They shouldn't be working on a Sunday. Aren't none of those men Christians?"

I explained that they needed to know as soon as possible whether the well had oil, but she didn't like that explanation.

I went back at the rig early Sunday morning and, sure enough, they were gonna try to bring in the well. A crowd had gathered to watch. Everybody wanted to be in on the excitement. My job was to keep the boiler fire supplied with firewood.

The men dropped a device called a bailer into the well to pull out the mud and water and make it easier for the oil to flow into the casing. They bailed for a couple of hours without any show of oil.

About eleven in the morning I heard a funny, low-pitched noise coming from the rig. All of a sudden the cable flew out of the hole, and pretty soon the bailer shot out too, and behind it was mud and water, then a roaring column of black liquid.

The roughnecks and driller jumped off the rig and ran to the south. They had warned me about the possibility of a fire if the well "gushed." I was on the other side of the rig, so I ran north. Well, the wind was from the south, and that spewing oil fell right down on me in big slick black drops. It soaked my hair and my clothes. I could hear the crowd in the clearing whoop and holler.

Mr. Cain turned a valve below the platform and diverted the oil into a tank. I walked back and saw a man come out of the crowd to talk to Mr. Cain. The man said, "I need to get Mother, Bill. She should be getting out of church about now."

Later, while we cleaned up, I asked Mr. Cain why the man wanted to bring his mother to the well. He said, "That was Malcolm Crim. His mother owns this land. She's gonna be one rich lady."

I also found out that because she owns the land her name goes on the well. Lou Della Crim #1, the second big well of the East Texas field.

8

Luke

They were wild times, Russ, those early months in 1931. The world we knew seemed to fall apart. People swarmed into here from all over the country—mostly men, but women and families too. They came on the freight trains. They drove cars. Some of 'em hitchhiked. They came because there was work here, getting that oil out of the ground.

Yeah, that truck driver wasn't even close about the size of the field. It turned out to be forty miles long, not thirteen. One huge field, the biggest oil field in the country! Four hundred square miles, and oil under every inch of it.

Overton was just outside the western boundary of the field, and boy, were we glad about that. Otherwise Overton might have ended up like Kilgore.

Kilgore. What a scene in those days. Seven hundred people in December, ten thousand people in January. Tent cities all over the place. Buildings going up everywhere—cheap houses, hotels, dormitories, machine shops, warehouses, hamburger stands, cafes, hospitals, grocery stores, sawmills, schools, honky-tonks, barbershops.

No paved streets either. You should have seen that place when it rained. The mud was so deep only mules could get through it. Big teams of mules, pulling those boilers and drill pipes and pumps through the mud, what a sight.

And what a smell. Nine thousand people living in tents, and no sewers. You didn't want to be downwind of those tents.

The derricks went up right there in town, hundreds of them. People tore down buildings to put in derricks, and stacked them right next to each other. About the only place you couldn't put a derrick was the middle of the street. Kilgore wasn't a town anymore, it was an oil camp, a thick forest of derricks.

And the people that came to that town. Good folks, oil workers and their families. And the not-so-good folks. Gamblers, cheats, hucksters, prostitutes, thieves, bootleggers, even murderers. Drawn by the money that flowed like oil.

I saw a lot of Kilgore in those days. Mr. Cain liked my work, and I stayed on as a roustabout. After the Crim well came in, we drilled up north of Kilgore, so I had to come through town every day to get to and from work. I dreaded when it rained. A couple of times I had to hire mules to pull my car out of the mud.

I worked the day shift, six in the morning 'til six at night. I looked forward to getting off work every day because Mom and Sis always had a nice meal for me when I got home.

Mom had lost about twenty pounds, but her condition seemed to have stabilized. She was tired by the time we sat down to eat, but she always waited up for me. That meal was very important for us.

One night we sat down to supper, and I got to talking about what a mess it was in Kilgore and how lucky we were to be in Overton. Marty piped up. "Can you drive us up to Kilgore to see the pajama ladies?"

Mom and I made eye contact, and Mom asked, "Where did you hear about those ladies?"

"In school. A boy was telling us he drove through there with his mom and dad, and they saw these ladies out in the street wearing beach pajamas."

I turned to Sis. "You don't want to be around those ladies. They're not nice."

Mom shook her head. "I knew that kind would show up. They just better not come to Overton."

Marty asked, "How are they not nice?"

I decided to answer her question, sort of. "They let men they don't know kiss them and stuff for money."

Mom raised her voice. "That's enough, Luke."

Marty giggled and asked how much money, but Mom put a firm end to that conversation.

◆ ◆ ◆

In early April I came home with good news, but didn't get the reaction I expected. After we sat down and had the prayer I told them, "I got a new job. Mr. Cain made me a floor man."

Mom frowned. "I sure don't like the sound of that. What do you mean?"

"Roughneck, on the floor of the rig. Take the drill string apart coming out of the hole and put it together going in. And here's the good news—seven bucks a day instead of the four I get now. We'll be able to pay our bills and save some too."

"That sounds dangerous, son, I hope you're careful."

"One other thing about it is, I have to start out on morning tour."

Marty asked, "What tower? The derrick?"

"Sounds like tower but it's spelled t-o-u-r. It means I work from six at night 'til six in the morning. New roughnecks have to start out on morning tour."

Well, Mom and Sis were unhappy to know that we wouldn't

have suppers together anymore, but I told them I'd get to see them in the afternoon before I left for the rig.

I got the hang of that roughneck job pretty quick. We had to work fast and hard when the driller pulled the pipe string out of the hole to change a bit or take a core, or going back in the hole after a bit change. But during the drilling itself we usually could rest. The hardest time was right before dawn. Lots of ways to get hurt on a drilling rig when you're tired. A good many roughnecks had lost a finger or two, and I came close myself a few times.

During that first summer on the rig I felt lucky to be working at night, because on many days the temperature got up to a hundred degrees. Of course I had to sleep during the day—not easy to do in sweat-soaked sheets, even with a fan blowing on me.

Mom or Sis always knocked on my door about two in the afternoon to wake me up. One August afternoon I heard the knock and then Marty's voice. "Hurry up and get dressed. We got news."

I dressed, shaved, and went to the sitting room. Marty jumped up from the chair. "Guess what? You won't have to go to work today. The governor shut down the oil field."

Mom nodded. "That's what we heard. He shut down the field and sent the National Guard in to enforce it. Said it's the only way to get oil prices back up."

I wasn't too surprised. I knew that Alfalfa Bill Murray, the Oklahoma governor, had already shut down the fields up there. So now Ross Sterling had followed suit.

Mom said, "I don't understand it. Don't people still need oil?"

"Yeah, but they're producing more than the oil companies need. That brings the price down. When the Joiner well came in, the price was about a dollar a barrel. Now it's down around a quarter, and going lower. That hurts everybody."

"Does it mean you're out of a job, son?"

"I don't know. Production and drilling are two different things. I think I'll go down to the barbershop and the garage and find out what the other guys have heard."

9

Luke

Russ, I gotta tell you about my Overton barber, a man named Al Fisher. Another fellow named Jim owned the shop, and the two of them worked sided by side. I don't even remember my first haircut, but I guess my dad must have decided that Al, not Jimmy, would cut my hair, so that's how it was all the years.

Al stood about five foot five, three inches shorter than his wife Doris. He had a round face and a smile that always seemed real natural. It was hard for that man to frown. I remember being in the shop a couple of times after somebody had died, and people would talk about the deceased person in somber tones, and Al would try to frown to fit the mood, but a few seconds later that smile would be back. It's like the mood couldn't change Al, but Al could change the mood. Sadness never hung around long in that shop.

Al liked to talk, and the funny thing was, he really didn't care whether you talked back or not. Now, there were some real quiet men in Overton. I remember a couple of my dad's friends who were that way. All business, never made small talk. Well, those men would go for their haircuts, and Al would talk to them. And you know what? When they realized they didn't *have* to say anything, they *would* talk. Al could bring out people that way.

When I was about eight years old, Al and Doris had their first baby, a girl they named Avis. Light brown hair, almost blonde. Boy, did we hear all about Avis when we got our haircuts. She did this. She ate that. She said a word. She stood up. She walked. We heard it all.

A year and a half later they had another girl, Darla, darker brown hair. We heard all about Darla *and* about Avis. A little while later, a third girl, Annie, a brunette.

The Fishers seemed like a pretty normal family at that time, nothing special. But then something happened when Avis was four years old.

We all heard the story, of course, a few days later. On Sunday morning the family had gone to church as usual, and Al and Doris had left the girls in the nursery. At the end of the hour Darla and Annie had gotten all tempered up, screaming, crying. After the service Al and Doris each picked up a girl, and Al told Avis to come along. Al and Doris walked home with the crying girls and assumed Avis was right behind them. Doris fed the little ones and tried to quiet them, then made dinner. Around one o'clock they called for Avis. But she wasn't in the house. Al looked everywhere. He went to the neighbors. They hadn't seen her. He started to worry, and walked back to the church. He heard piano music and followed it back to the nursery.

In that nursery was an old upright piano. On the bench were four hymnals from the sanctuary, two layers of two, and on top of the hymnals sat Avis. A hymnal was open in front of her, and she was playing a hymn, "We Gather Together." In four-part harmony.

Al told us he just listened, not believing it. But when she finished, he walked over and said, "How did you do that, darling?"

Avis looked up proudly and said, "Mrs. Baker showed me how the notes on the page go with the notes on the piano. I've tried to practice a little every week. Today I wanted to learn this hymn, so I stayed."

Al said, "But ... chords?"

Avis furrowed her brow and said, "There's a few I have trouble with, Daddy. My hands are too small. But if I kind of 'jump' my fingers real quick, I can make it sound like I hit the chord."

Al said he tried to be angry because she didn't follow them home, but he just couldn't pull it off. He told Avis that her mother was worried, and they needed to get home. So they took the hymn-books to the sanctuary and walked back to the house. And Al and Doris spent the afternoon wondering how a family of five on a barber's income could afford to buy a piano.

They found one, though, an old upright in a little bit better shape than the one in the nursery. And they found a teacher, a Mrs. Gaddis. Avis took lessons, and in two months she had finished the one-year beginner's course.

Darla and Annie must have liked the sound that piano made when Avis practiced. Darla started lessons at three, and she went through the beginner's course in six weeks. Mrs. Gaddis told Al and Doris that Darla might even have better keyboard skills than Avis, but Avis seemed to have a better understanding of the music. Al said he never knew what that meant.

Annie didn't start lessons until she was five, and she quit a year later. Al thought that maybe she just didn't like competing with her sisters. She stayed away for six months, then went back into it with gusto, like she wanted to catch up.

Three girls, all with great talent. Somebody even gave them nicknames—Melody, Harmony, and Rhythm. But the girls didn't like those names, so they faded away.

Al and Doris always said they didn't understand where the talent came from. Neither one of them ever played a musical instrument. But one day in the barbershop someone pointed out that Al's talents were in his hands. He worked his wonders, his service, with scissors and comb. Al liked that thought, and he said that Doris's talents were in her hands too. Doris was a great cook and seamstress. So Al decided that the girls were just using their God-given talent with hands in a different way. Musicians, cooks, and barbers, you need 'em all, Al used to tell us with a smile.

10

Luke

Al and Jim hadn't heard anything about whether the field shutdown included drilling or not, so I headed on down to the garage. Mr. Ross and Dewey seemed glad to see me, and Mr. Ross even offered me a job in the garage, which had more business than it could handle with the oil boom. That offer took some worry off my mind, and I thanked Mr. Ross and told him I'd let him know. But he hadn't heard anything about a drilling shutdown.

I decided the only way to find the answer was to drive out to my rig, a few miles north of Kilgore. I said good-bye to Dewey and Mr. Ross, turned to walk out of the work bay, and almost bumped into Vicky Orr.

Her look of surprise gave way to a big smile. "Hello, Luke."

"Hi, Vicky. Getting ready for your senior year?"

She nodded. "Any chance you'll be back? Make up what you missed? Maybe we could graduate at the same time."

"Can't do it. Mom has doctor bills. We need the money. Hey, why are you here in the garage?"

"Mother made me bring the car here to get new brake shoes. She said if I drive the car I need to help out with repairs."

We both turned to look at the car, and she said, "Luke, what do you do in the oil field? I talk to Marty now and then, and she tells me you're a roughneck, but I don't know what that means. Your neck doesn't look any different."

I laughed and found myself looking at *her* neck, then into her blue eyes. They were fixed on mine, and she still had that smile. An idea came to me.

"Vicky, I'm gonna drive out to my rig to find out if I have to work later. Want to come along? Maybe I can show you what a roughneck does."

That smile didn't waver a bit. "I'd love that, but I need to wait for Dewey to finish the brakes, then pay for the repair."

I turned back to the work bay. "Hey, Dewey, Vicky and I are going for a ride in my car. She'll come by and pay later, all right?"

"Sure thing. Be done when you get back."

A half-hour later we parked on a little rise overlooking the well, and I could see activity on the rig. I went to talk to the day driller, and he told me the governor's order didn't say anything about drilling. Business as usual.

I told Vicky I'd have to work later, and she pointed to the rig. "What's happening up there?"

I opened the car door. "There's a little breeze out here. Let's go stand in the shade of that oak tree, and I'll tell you what's going on."

We walked under a big oak about forty yards from the rig. "Right now they're drilling," I told her. "Should have about twenty-nine hundred feet of pipe in the hole. We were at twenty-seven hundred feet last night, and we're averaging about three hundred feet a day. Got another five hundred feet or so to go before we hit oil sand."

"Can I ask a dumb question?"

"Sure, but I bet it's not dumb."

"How do they get the dirt out of the hole?"

"Mud. See that flexible hose on the top of the kelly, that square pipe? Mud gets pumped through it down the hollow drill pipe and out through the drill bit at the bottom of the pipe string. The mud picks up what the drill bit cuts and takes it up to the surface between the drill pipe and the wall of the hole. Mud cools the drill bit too, otherwise it'd get real hot from friction."

"Are those roughnecks standing up there?"

"Yep, two roughnecks, floor men. The driller's the man with his hand on the lever. And the derrick man, that's the roughneck up high on the thribble board. In a minute they're gonna need to put on a new joint, and you'll see how it's done."

I glanced at Vicky. Her mouth had a twist. "The what board?" she asked.

"Thribble board. Three pipe joints high."

She laughed and put her hand on her forehead.

I said, "What's so funny?"

She shook her head. "You men and your words." She grinned and laughed again.

A couple of minutes later the crew started to put on a new joint of drill pipe, and I explained it to Vicky.

"Watch, they're putting the elevators on the kelly to pull it out. The elevators are what's hanging from the traveling block, that pulley thing.

"Okay, now they've got the kelly and the top two joints out, then they'll put in the slips to hold the string, see that? The slips are big enough to go around the pipe but the ends of the pipe are bigger, that's how it's held in place. Now they're putting the tongs on the second joint, to keep the kelly and the top joints from rotating. See, the driller's turning the rotary table and the top joints are unscrewing from the string.

"All right, now they've got the kelly and the top joints loose, so they'll put 'em in the rathole for a minute while they get the next joint on."

Vicky burst into laughter. She looked up at me with tears in her eyes. I smiled. She giggled a bit longer, then wiped her eyes and said, "I worked with tongs one time."

"Huh?"

"Picked up a pickle."

She laughed, and I laughed. Then she said, "I know about slips, too." That brought more laughter. We kept looking at each other, and we couldn't stop laughing. Finally we did stop, but then her lips started to tremble, and she said, "rathole," and we were at it again. We must have laughed for two minutes straight. We'd try to stop, but then we'd look at each other and start over.

Finally we quieted down, and Vicky turned toward the rig. "So that square pipe is the kelly, huh?"

"Yeah."

"I've got a cousin named Kelly." She grinned and I grinned back.

She was silent for a moment, but then she looked at the rig and said, "But why is the kelly square, Luke?"

"The kelly's square so the rotary table can torque the string."

"Torque?"

"Give me your arm, I'll show you."

She offered up her left arm and I put my thumb and forefinger around her wrist and rotated it through a right angle. "See, your wrist is kind of flat and I can use that flat surface to apply pressure and rotate it."

I looked into those blue eyes and they looked back, bigger than before. She wasn't smiling.

I slid my hand toward her elbow. "Down here, your arm is more round, and it's harder to rotate. That's why the kelly's square—four flat surfaces make it easier to get rotational force, called torque."

I let go of her arm. She said, "Can I try it?" She reached for my arm, but not the one nearest her. She reached across and took hold of my left wrist. I turned and faced her. She put her fingers around my wrist and gave it a little twist. She said the word "torque" very softly, and nodded.

Then she slid her hand down my arm, just like I had done to her. She said, "Got to have big, strong arms to be a roughneck, don't you?"

I nodded.

Her eyes went from my eyes to my mouth. I saw that her mouth was opened a little bit. I knew she wanted me to kiss her. But I didn't do it. I just looked at her. Then I said, "Let's go back to Kilgore and get a soda pop."

She smiled, gave a little sigh, patted my arm and said, "That's a wonderful idea."

Maybe I should have kissed her. I sometimes wonder how things might be different if I had. But I was afraid of her that afternoon. She was pretty and smart and bound for college, and I was just a roughneck.

11

Luke

The governor opened the field for production in September, but set an "allowable." Only so much oil could be taken from each well, to keep prices up. Folks called it "proration." Of course, some of the oil companies and landowners didn't like that, so they cheated. Built hidden pipelines. Tried to sneak the oil out in trucks at night. The National Guard stayed in the field, and they were kept pretty busy trying to track down all the "hot oil," as they called it.

Proration didn't affect me, since drilling wasn't limited. Lots of new wells, new crews. In late 1931 I got the news I'd been waiting for on a Saturday night and couldn't wait to tell Mom and Sis about it.

I got home that Sunday morning and found Mom sitting up in bed and Sis dressed for Sunday school. We gathered in the bedroom, and I gave them the good news.

"Day tour. Starting next week. Work days and sleep nights, like people are supposed to."

Marty grinned and clapped, and Mom patted my hand and said, "That's wonderful, honey."

"Yep, I've paid my dues. They're still drilling more wells, and there's a lot of new roughnecks, so us experienced guys get the day tour if we want it."

"That is good news. And we need some, we're worried about something."

"Oh, what, Mom?"

She sighed. "There's something going on with the Erwins. Something's happening, and they won't tell us what it is."

"How do you know?"

"There's a little change in the way Rachel talks to me. She still comes over every day, but any time we start talking about things a little in the future, she changes the subject. It's hard for me to put my finger on, but Marty's noticed things too."

"Yes," Marty said. "Rie even told me she has a big secret, and she can't tell me even though I'm her best friend. I tried to guess her secret. I guessed things like new baby, new car, and she kept shaking her head. Then I said, 'new house,' and she didn't shake her head, she just put her hand over her mouth."

Mom said, "Anyway, they've invited us for supper tonight."

"Good, maybe they'll tell us what's going on. You gonna try to make it to church today, Mom?"

"No, I don't feel up to it. Marty's going with Rie to their church."

I turned to Sis. "Marty's gonna turn into a Baptist if she keeps going with Rie."

She shook her head. "No, I won't turn into a Baptist. I don't want to get dunked in the river."

When we were all seated at the table that night, Tom told us they were moving four miles down the road to a little community called London.

Mom looked stunned, but I almost laughed. I thought he was joking. London was just a country intersection, a dot on a map.

Tom cleared up the confusion. "Luke, you know the area north of London is smack dab in the middle of the oil field, right?"

"Yeah, they call it the 'fairway.' The oil sand's thickest there."

"Lots of new activity in that area. Wells, pumping stations, pipelines, tank farms, loading racks, compressors, gasoline plants. The oil companies are putting in camps for the workers and their families. They're building a new school, just north of London. Two schools, really, primary and high school. I was offered the job of principal of the primary school. I took it. We need to live near the school. We're having a house built in the new community."

Mom turned to Rachel with a frown of fear, and Sis seemed ready to cry. But Rachel smiled and said, "And we want you to move there with us."

Tom nodded. "Do it, Luke. You can get a good price for your house. Rachel and Wilma need to be close. Marty and Rie need to go to the new school together. It's gonna be a top-notch school. Build a little house near us."

Mom and I just stared at each other, but Sis grinned and said, "Yes!"

We thought about it over the next few days. Marty begged us to move. Wanted a house with her own room—she and Mom had been sharing a room up to then.

I couldn't think of any reason not to do it. I worked in the oil field, and London sat in the middle of the field. But could Mom leave the house she'd lived in for twenty-two years, the house where Marty and I had been born?

She surprised me by telling me she wanted to move, to be near

Rachel. Told me that Marty and I were what was left of Daddy, not the house.

We did it, Russ. Followed the Erwins to London. Sold the place in Overton and hired a man to build a house with three small bedrooms, one street over from the Erwins, about a mile north of where the new school would be. Our lot even had a shade tree, an oak, in the back yard.

A few other folks from Overton made the move to London. Ben Halley, the Overton banker, moved so his son Tim could attend the new school. Then one night in February, Sis ran into the house and yelled, "Annie's coming! Annie's coming! Her dad's gonna open his own shop in London! My two best friends and I are going to the new school!"

I smiled and turned to Mom. "That is good news. I won't have to drive back to Overton for my haircuts. Al told me he always wanted to have his own shop. Bet he'll do real good there. The oil field's full of men, and they all need haircuts now and then."

"Luke, what's gonna happen to Mom?"

Sis asked me that while we cooked supper together one night a couple of weeks after the move. Ever since the move, Mom had stayed in bed almost all day.

"She's a fighter, Sis. She'll come through."

Sis stared at the beans she was stirring and said, "I don't remember Daddy."

"You were just two."

"I worry about you out on those drilling rigs. They can burn. I've read about it."

"I'm real careful."

"It would be very bad for us if something happened to you."

"Nothing will."

◆ ◆ ◆

One night we heard a knock while we cooked, and Marty went to the door. "Vicky. You've come to see us." I went to greet Vicky. She held a dish wrapped in tinfoil.

"Luke, here's a housewarming present for you and your family. A chocolate pie. I baked it myself." She beamed the same bright-eyed smile I remembered from that summer afternoon.

I said, "You're very nice to do this. How's your cousin Kelly?"

She laughed. "You've got a good memory. Gee, that was so long ago."

Her tone made me think she wasn't real happy that I hadn't talked to her since that day. Of course I didn't have any time to date girls, what with my work hours and Mom's illness. Also, I was building a front porch for the house in my little spare time.

I said, "That pie smells wonderful. And you're going to stay and eat supper with us and have some afterward?"

She glanced at the table. "Oh, no, Luke, you didn't prepare for four people."

"No arguments, you're staying. Marty, show her the house while I finish up in the kitchen. Mom will be glad to see you, Vicky."

When we sat down to supper, Mom put on her robe and joined us.

I felt Vicky's eyes on me many times during the meal. At one point she said, "Is there anything you can't do, Luke? You wire houses for electricity. You fix cars. You drill oil wells. You cook. You build front porches."

Marty grinned. "Nope. There's nothing my brother can't do."

I said, "Hey, I can't play the piano."

In a serious tone Vicky said, "I bet if you wanted to you could. You know, I really admire people who can do lots of things well. I don't meet many … men like that."

At the end of the meal I served the pie, and after my first bite

I put down my fork. "There's something else I can't do. Make a pie this good."

Mom and Sis chimed their agreement. Vicky smiled and said, "Want me to teach you how?"

"No, just keep bringing them over. We like your company too."

She reached over and patted my arm. "What a sweet thing to say."

Mom and Marty exchanged a quick glance. I said, "But, I guess we won't be seeing much of you after this fall. Going off to Southern Methodist University. A college girl. Bet you graduate and get a job in a big city, Dallas or Houston."

She shook her head. "I'm an East Texas girl. East Texas needs teachers just as much as the big cities do. Yes, I'm going to college, but I'll be home for summers and holidays, so you'll see me … if you want to. Could you ever leave East Texas, Luke?"

"Got no reason to. I'm an oil field man, and this field's gonna be around a long, long time."

After Vicky left, Marty came to me and said, "Wow, does she like you."

I nodded.

"Why don't you ask her out?"

"'Cause I might start to like her. Then she'd go off to college and meet a college man and get married."

"*I'd* rather marry an oil field man than a college man."

An oil man doesn't forget words like that, Russ.

12

Russ

*D*uring the three days it took us to finish up Widow Daniels's yard, Luke talked so much I hardly got a chance to sing. Sometimes he'd reach an obvious stopping point, the end of some episode, and I'd breathe a sigh of relief and look forward to the quiet, but then he'd start again. It was like the story had boiled up, gushed up, inside of him, and he had to pour it out to keep from exploding. But *why* did he feel such a need? I still didn't know why, and a vague worry still nagged me.

I couldn't help but listen, even though I rarely looked at him or acknowledged anything he said. I learned about the man himself, but also about Marty and others whose names graced the headstones. And I longed to know more. Names and dates on a headstone don't tell you much. Of course, when a lot of the markers say Died March 18, 1937, that does tell you something very terrible, but nothing about the people—what they were like, who they loved, who loved them.

We hauled dirt for two days, then put down topsoil and laid St. Augustine grass on top. We put in a couple of pecan trees and some shrubs. Built steps from the sidewalk up to yard level. Mrs. Daniels praised our work.

On that last day a man drove by several times and finally stopped, came over to me, said he liked what we had done and wondered if we could do the same thing to his yard.

Luke, about ten feet away, heard the question. Before I could speak, he said, "I can stay, Russ." I knew he wasn't through with his story.

It seemed right to celebrate finishing the job with a special meal. "Luke, how does catfish for supper sound?"

"Mighty fine."

"Good. Supper will be a little late though. We have to catch the fish."

"Where?"

"Sabine River, south of Gladewater. Fellow up there lets me use his rowboat. We'll try for five fish so I can share with my neighbors."

◆ ◆ ◆

The road down to the river from the highway, shadowed by ancient oak, sweet gum, and ash, seemed narrower than when I'd last driven it. The dense vegetation fought to reclaim its rightful territory. I worried about coming back out after dark, but there was no retreating. Finally we made it to the little clearing, and I saw the rowboat in its usual spot.

We loaded up, and Luke pushed off and rowed us upstream a couple of hundred yards. At a sharp bend we tied to a willow tree and let out some rope, which kept the boat in a steady position twenty feet out from shore.

I enjoy the sounds of the river at evening, the croaks and chirps of the bullfrogs and crickets. I looked forward to a couple of hours of quiet fishing. Luke had talked so much during the day I figured he could do with some silence also, to rest his voice if nothing else.

The first hour passed as I'd hoped. Neither of us said a word, except when we caught the two fish and strung them. Then things changed. And it was all my fault.

The sun was an hour gone, and the moon had yet to rise. I looked up at the star-flecked black sky and for some reason started to sing.

> Soon as dies the sunset glory,
> Stars of heaven shine out above,
> Telling still the ancient story,
> Their Creator's changeless love.

I hummed the refrain, and Luke said, "Russ?"

"Yeah?"

"You know hymns. You sing hymns. You have perfect pitch. You hit the high notes and low notes both. You go to church. But you've never sung in the choir. Why not?"

Well, I'd brought it on myself. But I was ready. Question and answer, end of discussion. "Someone tells a choir what to sing. I sing what I feel like singing."

"You said you worked in a hospital before. Whereabouts was that hospital?"

I held my pole and prayed a catfish would bite. I retreated into silence, hoping Luke would take the hint and shut up. But he didn't.

"Then you moved to Turnertown. You weren't running from the law, were you?"

Silence, except for the distant howl of a dog from upriver.

"Or maybe it was a woman. You were running from something, the law or a woman. So you moved to a little community where nobody knew you. Didn't use your real name, of course. But I gotta tell you, Russ, that 'Smith' is a pretty weak alias. You coulda done better."

I said, "Luke, you talked all day. You gonna talk all night too?"

That comment shut him up for a while. Twenty minutes later he hauled in a fat catfish, strung it up, rebaited his hook with a catalpa worm, and lowered it into the water. Then he said, "You were there when it happened, weren't you?"

I could have pretended ignorance, but saw no point in it. "No, sir."

Even in the dark I could feel his eyes on me.

"The day after?"

When I didn't respond he said, "Hospital man. Doctor. Doctor Smith. You came the day after. You worked on the injured. What's wrong with that? Why don't you just tell me?"

"That's not right. I wasn't there the day after." I wiped my brow with my sleeve and listened to the thump of my heartbeat.

"You were there, Russ. Maybe the next day. Maybe later. But you were there. You know where all the graves are. What are you hiding?"

Like a cornered animal, I looked for a way out. But I couldn't find one. Finally I said, "Let's just enjoy the night."

He grunted and kept quiet until he pulled in the fourth catfish a few minutes later. I told him I was hungry, and we'd settle for four fish. He untied us, and we drifted downstream to the truck. We drove home, cleaned and fried the fish, and ate our supper. In glorious silence.

The next day we hauled crossties. Back and forth, Henderson to Tyler. Over the roar of the truck's engine Luke continued his story.

13

Luke

December 1932. Sis woke me up frantic with joy one morning before dawn and dragged me to the sitting room. Snowflakes fell like big balls of cotton through the glow of the porch light, and blanketed the earth.

Marty had never seen snow before. She was beside herself. "I don't want to go to school. I want to play in the snow."

"I bet they don't have school. Buses can't get around in this."

She whooped and clapped. "Luke, stay home from work and play with us."

Well, I hadn't told Mom and Sis, but I *did* plan to stay home that day, and it didn't have anything to do with the snow. The governor had shut down the field again, not because of cheap oil, but to run a test. The pressure at the bottom of the wells had gotten low, and if it went much lower the oil wouldn't flow to the surface on its own. So it was decided to shut down all wells, and drilling too, and see if the pressure went back up. If it did, there would have to be some new rules set on production.

I'd be off work for a whole week, and I'd planned to surprise

Mom and Sis with the news. When I told Sis I could play in the snow with her, she was thrilled.

At breakfast Sis gazed out the window at the gray dawn and said, "I wish I could talk to Rie right now." Mom smiled.

Marty said, "Luke, do you remember when we got electricity at the house in Overton? Remember how that all started?"

"Yeah, I remember."

"It started when I asked you if you knew anything about electricity. Remember that?"

"Yeah."

"Well, I've got another question for you."

"What?"

"Do you know anything about telephones?"

Mom winked. "Tom's getting them a telephone for Christmas."

I pondered the news. "But their telephone won't be any good if they can't talk to their friends, will it? So I guess we'll have to get a telephone too."

Marty's mouth dropped open. She jumped out of her chair and ran around the table to hug me. "This is gonna be the best Christmas ever!"

I held Sis and turned to Mom. "Is it all right?"

She patted my arm. "You're sweet to ask, honey, but you know it's your decision. And you've made me just as happy as Marty, I promise."

I felt a great love for my little family at that moment, Russ.

I played with Sis and her friends for a few hours that morning. We built a snowman and fought with snowballs. Then I left them to play on their own and tromped through the white powder to the barbershop. I followed a trail of footprints that converged on the door.

Al had put in two barber chairs when he built the shop, and that turned out to be a wise decision, because his business grew. A new barber, Pete, now worked the second chair.

The shop rang with voices that morning. Everyone had something to say about the snow or the field shutdown.

A little table next to the door normally held a magazine or two, but now I saw a bowl with coins, mostly nickels and dimes but a few pennies. Taped to the table next to the bowl was a picture of a piano, cut from a newspaper. When my turn came for a haircut I asked Al about it.

Al clipped as he spoke. "To tell you the whole story I need to back up a little, Luke. You heard about how Avis did in that regional piano competition in Dallas last summer, right?"

I grinned. "Al, how could I help hearing about it? I get my haircuts here, don't I?"

"Just refreshing your memory. I also told you about the state competition in San Antonio last month, right?"

"Sure. She won the North Texas contest, so she got to go to the state contest. Y'all went down on the train and stayed with a preacher's family. She didn't win the state competition though."

Al shook his head. "Nope. I need to tell you a little more about that day. The program started about two in the afternoon, in a big auditorium in downtown San Antonio. There were five kids in the competition, one from each big region of the state. They each played for about thirty to forty-five minutes. Oh, were they good. I have no idea how anybody could judge that one was better than another.

"Avis was the next-to-last performer. She played a Beethoven sonata, and it was just perfect, as usual. I know that sonata very well from listening to her practice it week after week. I knew she hadn't missed a note.

"The audience clapped loudly when she finished. But when she took her bow, I didn't see the smile I expected. In Dallas she had a big joyous smile when she bowed, but in San Antonio her smile was thinner.

"When they were all finished, a man came out an announced that the boy from Houston, representing South Texas, had won. He had played right before Avis. We were disappointed, but not too much. Just getting to the state competition was a great honor. I didn't expect Avis to be upset.

"We got on a train around seven o'clock for the long ride back to Overton. Avis sat by herself, with her coat on the seat beside her, like she didn't want anyone sitting there. We were all tired, so I didn't pay much attention.

"I drifted off to sleep around nine, and woke up about an hour or so later. Annie and Darla were across the aisle from us, both asleep. Avis, in the seat in front of us, was awake, staring out the window into the darkness. I tapped her on the shoulder, leaned up and whispered, 'You played that sonata perfectly. You should have won.'

"She jerked her head toward me and said loudly, 'No I didn't. And the boy that won, I promise you he doesn't have to practice on a thirty-year-old upright.' Then she turned around and stared out the window. And I felt a great sadness come over me, and a feeling of helplessness.

"We got back to Overton about one in the morning and went right to bed, exhausted. An hour or so later, I don't know what time it was, a hand on my arm pulled me out of a sound sleep. Avis knelt next to the bed in her nightgown, sobbing, her face wet with tears. I mumbled, 'What's wrong, honey?'

"'I'm sorry,' she sobbed.

"'For what?'

"'For what I said to you on the train. I am so sorry, Daddy. I am here to ask you to forgive me for those horrible words. I can't sleep.'

"I took her hand in mine and said, 'Darling, of course I forgive you. You don't even have to ask.'

"She shook her head quickly. 'No, Daddy, that's not right. I *do* have to ask. I do. Now, please tell me you forgive me because I asked you to.'

"I squeezed her hand and said, 'Because you asked me, and because I love you, I forgive you.'

"Her face changed. She smiled through the tears. She kissed me on the forehead and said, 'Now I can sleep.' She tiptoed out of the room.

"When she was gone, Doris rolled over and said, 'I heard that. I heard what she said on the train too. She did real good to apologize, but ...'

"'But what?'

"'But somewhere, somehow, we've gotta get another piano. That's tomorrow's problem though. Tonight we rest. Go to sleep.'

"God gave us rest that night. And Avis was her usual cheerful self the next day. She never said any more about the old piano. But Doris and I couldn't ignore her comment on the train. Two weeks ago we went to see Mrs. Gaddis, the girls' teacher.

"Mrs. Gaddis started off by telling us that all three girls had great talent. No real news there. Doris and I nodded and thanked her. Then she got real serious. She told us Avis was being held back in her progress, and Darla and Annie would soon have the same problem. It was the piano, she said. The keys had no resistance. No 'dynamic range,' she called it. Pianists need to vary the volume of sounds over a wide range, and with that old piano, it just wasn't possible.

"Could the piano be fixed? No. What do we do? She nodded

and showed me the picture taped to the table. With fear in my heart I asked the price, and cringed when I heard it. Hundreds of dollars. 'That's for a good used one,' she said.

"Mrs. Gaddis left after promising to help us search for a piano if we wanted to pursue it. Doris and I almost cried. How could we ever come up with that kind of money?

"A couple of days later I told Ben Halley the story during his haircut. Ben told me the community needed music. 'Put out a bowl,' he said. 'Tell the men what it's for. It'll take a while, but we'll help you get that piano.' And that's the story, Luke."

I thought: He will never get that much money. But then I remembered the first service at our new church, held in an oil company warehouse. Avis Fisher, twelve years old, sat at an upright piano and played the hymns while we sang.

I dropped a dime in that bowl as I walked out of the barbershop.

◆ ◆ ◆

Sis and I had watched Mom struggle with her illness for three years. Mom hated the term "invalid," and fought hard to rise above it. She got dressed every day, even though she rarely left the house. She cooked, even though cooking tired her. She sat with Sis and me at our meals. She forced herself to go to church on Sunday.

What we called "spells" came and went over the years. Loss of appetite, extreme fatigue, heavy coughing. In the past, those episodes had lasted a week or so. But in late 1933 she came down with a spell, and two weeks passed, then three, with no recovery. She shrunk to a terrible thinness, and her desperate, labored breathing rattled through our sleepless nights. The doctor came, but told us he could do nothing.

Rachel, her one true friend, kept her company most of the

daylight hours. One day in mid-January I got home from work, and Rachel met me at the door. "Go to her now," Rachel said.

Mom seemed a part of the bed itself. I sat and held her hand. "Come close," she moaned, and I leaned over.

Her words came in slow, painful whispers. "Luke, you're a man today. You're twenty-one years old."

She was right, I realized. Sis and I had been so worried and exhausted we hadn't even thought about it. But as desperately ill as Mom was, she had known.

"Luke," she whispered, "age doesn't make a man. You've been a man for the last eight years."

I caressed her forehead.

She whispered, "Marty came from God, Luke. I'm so happy you love her so much. Watch over her after I leave."

A tear rolled down my cheek. "Don't leave, Mom. Stay with us."

She said, "I'm going to heaven. Watch over my little girl."

"No. We want you here."

She struggled to lift her hand to my wrist. "I'm tired." Her last words came to me in a whispered moan. The hand fell from my wrist. She died the next day.

We held her service in the new church sanctuary. Avis Fisher played some of her favorite hymns, the people sang, and the pastor gave a short eulogy. We buried her in the cemetery you know so well, Russ, Pleasant Hill. I reckon you've walked past her grave on many a day.

A week later Sis and I sat in Judge Scott's office in Henderson, and the judge asked me a question: "Luke, do you want to take care of Marty?"

I said, "Yes, I do."

Marty put her hand on my arm, and I turned to her. I saw tears and a glorious smile. Then I remembered Mom's words, for me to watch over Marty, and I figured that Sis's smile beamed all the way up to heaven.

After my guardianship was made official, the judge shook my hand. "Keep her from harm, Luke."

14

Luke

In early summer of 1934 I met a strawberry blonde at a strawberry stand. Pretty funny, huh, Russ? I thought so myself at the time. I don't laugh about it now.

I'd stopped at the stand on my way home from work. Thought I'd surprise Sis with strawberries for dessert that night. I bought the berries, headed back to my car, and heard a starter motor cranking. I could tell the car had a problem, so I walked over and said, "Ma'am, don't run down your battery. If you like I'll try to see what the trouble is."

Early twenties, I guessed. Blonde hair with a reddish tint, brown eyes, and a complexion like a doll's. No ring on her left hand.

She said "Thanks" to my offer. I lifted the hood, pulled off a plug wire, and told her to crank it for a few seconds. Went to my car for tools, popped the distributor cap, and pulled out the corroded points. I told her there was a parts store in Kilgore and that I'd drive up and get what she needed if she wanted to wait.

She smiled. "I'll ride with you. I got to pay for the part, don't I?" I opened the door for her, and she stepped out. She was tall, about five-eight, but not thin. Had it in all the right places, Russ.

We drove to Kilgore and talked quite a bit on the way and back. Her name was Carol Tippitt, and she waited tables at Mattie's, a big dance hall up on the road to Longview. Lived with her mother.

She thanked me when I got her engine running again, and told me she'd like to repay me. Offered to buy me a drink or two if I'd meet her at Mattie's on her night off, the following Monday. I figured Marty was old enough to stay by herself for part of the night, so I said yes. I'd never been out with a real looker like Carol.

What a night that turned out to be. I won't tell you everything that happened, Russ, 'cause you're old, and you might have a heart attack. But I'll tell you how it started.

We met in the club parking lot. She had on a light blue dress, big silver earrings, high heels, and red lipstick. Man, did she look good in those heels.

We didn't have to pay a cover charge since Carol worked there. A good-sized crowd filled the place—some folks were sitting, some standing, some dancing to the music of a four-piece band up front.

We found a table. A waitress came, and I guess she and Carol were friends because they chatted for a bit before the gal took our order. She came back in a minute with a couple of colas, and I reached for my billfold to pay, but Carol said she'd get the first round.

Carol pulled a half-pint bottle from her purse and poured into the two cola glasses until they almost overflowed. Then she stirred them both with her index finger. She picked up her glass and told me to do the same. She clinked her glass to mine and said, "To strawberries and broken cars."

She winked and sipped her drink. I took a swallow and cringed. That drink tasted awful.

Carol put down her glass and grinned at me. "Luke, tell me something. Be honest. Is that the first time you've had a drink with alcohol in it?"

Well, at least I knew what caused the bad taste. I said, "Yeah, I guess it is."

"That's the way it was with me the first time. But you get used to it. Just sip it, don't take big swallows. It'll taste okay in a while. That's a good brand of bourbon."

She took a pack from her purse, pulled out a cigarette, and popped it in her mouth. She handed me a book of matches. "Light me."

I did, and she asked if I smoked, and I said no.

She said, "I don't smoke a lot. Mom won't let me do it in the house. But I like smokes with my drinks."

Fifteen minutes later my glass was half empty, and hers was empty. I felt warm and relaxed. Carol ordered more setups, and when they arrived, she topped hers off with bourbon and took a swallow. I couldn't take my eyes off her.

"Thank goodness they got rid of that stupid Prohibition law last year. You couldn't even find a decent place to go have a drink. You had to go to these dives, and half the time the cops would come in and raid the place right in the middle of your evening. Man, I got tired of that. Hey, when I finish this one I want you to dance with me, Luke."

"I might have forgotten how. Haven't danced since tenth grade."

"Don't worry. If you've forgotten how I'll teach you. I'll teach you everything you need to know." She leaned forward and tapped on the back of my left hand with two fingers. Her face glowed. I moved my chair closer. I wanted to breathe in her perfume.

We danced. I bought her more cigarettes. We danced. I bought her more colas. I finished my second drink. Incredibly, her beauty, her charm, seemed to increase as the night wore on. I wanted to dance, slowly, holding her close, all of her.

Between dances she told me about her brothers, one in prison for theft and the other a welder in the oil field. She told me about her aunts, her uncles, her cousins, her travels, her schools, her girlhood. The way she told stories made everything seem funny. I hadn't laughed so much in a long time.

At one point she rubbed her hand through my hair and said, "You've got charm, Luke. A big, handsome roughneck with charm. I like that. Now, we've got a little problem. My bottle's empty. I'm enjoying this night. I want it to go on. Go buy us another bottle."

"Huh?"

"They don't sell liquor here. Drive up toward Longview. There's a liquor store about two miles up the road. Get a half-pint of bourbon, same brand as mine. Please?" She brushed my chin with a finger.

I drove to that store very carefully. I was back in twenty minutes. Carol had the setups ready and topped off our glasses.

We danced very close after that, cheek to cheek. We drank, and ate sandwiches, and looked at each other in silence while we ate.

Finally we walked out of Mattie's, arm in arm. I had a need, a want, but didn't know how to ask her. I didn't have to. Carol knew what I wanted, and she wanted the same thing. I won't burn your ears with details, Russ. But Carol did what she had told me she would do. She taught me everything I needed to know.

◆ ◆ ◆

In the fall of that year I got a real shock, but a pleasant one, when I got to work one morning. I climbed up to the rig floor and saw a new roughneck talking to my normal partner, Bud, near the rotary table. Ken Kincaid, the day driller, stood by the drawworks and motioned me over.

"Who's the new guy, Ken?"

"Name's Mac. He'll be working the floor with Bud from now on."

I felt a chill. "Anything wrong with my work?"

"Not at all. Tell me something. We're at 3,200 feet right now. How far down to Austin Chalk?"

I didn't have any idea why he was asking me. He was the driller, he should know that himself. But I started thinking out loud.

"Well, the last well we drilled was about a half-mile west of here. We hit the chalk at 3,460, if I remember right. The formation slopes up, west to east, about 40 feet every mile. So I'd guess we'll hit the caprock at about 3,440 feet, which means we got about 240 feet to go."

"From the top of the caprock to the Woodbine, how thick?"

"This far east, about 150, 160 feet."

"How many roller bits to get through 150 feet of chalk?"

"The bits we're using, probably two."

"Pretty good. Now, Bud and Mac, I could ask them those same questions, and I'd get blank stares. You're different. You pay attention. You try to understand what's going on around you."

I shrugged.

"You've paid your dues, Luke. Ready to learn the driller's job?"

I stared at him for a moment. "I sure am, friend."

"Good. You'll start to train with me today. Lots to learn, and it'll take a while, but you can do it."

Sis was waiting for me in the swing when I got home. I hopped up on the porch and sat down beside her. "Guess what."

"Hey, you're not as dirty today. Why not?"

"'Cause I didn't roughneck. I got a new job. I'm a driller trainee. I train with another man for a few weeks, then I'm in charge of the rig. And here's the best part—once I'm a driller, I get ten bucks a day."

"Wow. We'll be rich. I'm real proud of you." She put both arms around my neck. "Hey, you don't smell as bad either."

I laughed. "Well, I still got to clean up for supper. What are we having?"

"Stew, beans, and cobbler. I've got the beans cooking now, and the stew and cobbler we'll just heat up."

"Sure appreciate you helping me cook, Sis."

"You work hard. I like cooking for you."

During supper Sis didn't say much but kept a smile. Finally I said, "Okay, Sis. You've got something on your mind. I see that smile. What are you thinking about?"

She pretended to chew on a fingernail. "Well ..."

"Well, what?"

"Well, you did say you'll be making more money, right?"

"Yes ... uh, oh, I think I shouldn't have started this."

"And ... next month's my birthday, right?"

"Yeah, your eleventh. I think I'm in trouble."

"Remember how we got electricity, and how we got a telephone? How it all started with me asking you a question?"

"Now I know I'm in trouble."

"Well, I have another question for you."

I put fingers in both ears and closed my eyes, but Marty pulled the finger from my right ear, leaned close and whispered, "Do you know anything about radios?"

Two months later I was a driller. The roughnecks, the roustabouts, the cables, the chains, the drums, the pipes all moved at my command. I stood on top of the world. But that didn't last long.

Early in '35 we spudded in our first well in Upshur County, near the northwest edge of the field. Everything went fine for the first couple of weeks, until we got down to the caprock, or what I thought was the caprock.

It happened around four-thirty on a frigid afternoon. I noticed that the drill string had slowed vertically, so I assumed we'd hit the chalk, the hard limestone. I figured to drill another half-hour or so, then pull the string to put on a new bit and let the evening tour go back in the hole.

About ten minutes later I got a real surprise. The string moved fast again, like we were in sand or shale. But I knew the caprock was at least 140 feet thick, even as far west and north as we were. It was a puzzle, and I didn't like puzzles out on the rig.

I decided to stop drilling but to keep circulating the mud so I could check the cuttings a few minutes later. I brought the rotary table to a stop.

Bud saw it before I did. He yelled, and I saw raw fear in his eyes. The pipe string was coming out of the hole on its own.

I jerked my head upward and saw the derrick man jump for the safety rope. I turned back to the floor men and screamed, "Jump!" but they didn't hear me. They were flat on their faces next to the rotary table. The string moved upward, and the wellhead roared.

I didn't have time to save the floor men. I turned to jump and a tremendous force slammed me in the back. I flew off the rig and landed in the slush pit.

Deep in mud, I couldn't breathe. I didn't know which way was up. I stuck out both arms and felt my right hand go out of the mud into hot air. My feet found the bottom of the pit, and I pushed. My face rose above the mud, and I turned toward the rig and got a vision of hell.

Massive orange flames blasted from the wellhead, reaching up through the crown block. Huge clouds of black smoke boiled above the flames. And what a sound. That roar was like a bomb going off, but continuous. My eardrums felt like they were gonna break. I watched the rig melt, disintegrate. My face burned like it was inside the flames.

To cool my head I dipped it into the mud. The far edge of the pit, the earthen berm, twenty feet distant, was my only hope. I clawed my way forward in great pain. I could only go a few feet at a time before stopping to rest. Finally I made it to the berm. But the pit had a steep slope. My legs felt like they were sealed in concrete.

I tried to inch my way up the slope. Only one arm worked, and neither leg. The heat roasted me. I knew I couldn't make it to the top. I closed my eyes, and thought about Sis, and knew the Erwins would take care of her.

I heard a man's voice. "Over here!" I opened my eyes and saw a pair of boots.

A half-hour later I lay in a Gladewater hospital where they told me I had two broken ribs, a broken arm, and a bruised spinal column.

Ken Kincaid showed up. He told me the derrick man and roustabout were okay, but the two floor men and the boiler man were dead, burned up.

I felt sick to my stomach. I had been in charge, and three men had died. I told Kincaid about Bud and Mac falling over before the explosion. He said the gas had knocked them out.

"But Ken, with that much gas coming out of the hole I should have smelled something. I didn't. My eyes got watery, but I didn't smell a thing."

He shook his head. "Nothing to smell. This is a low-sulfur field. Down on the Gulf Coast you'd smell that sulfurated gas for sure. But up here it's just methane and the light ends. No odor."

Marty and the Erwins showed up a few minutes after Kincaid left. Sis ran up, put her arms around me, sobbed and said three words, over and over: "Don't go back."

15

Luke

I couldn't go back to the rigs, Russ. Everyone told me it wasn't my fault, that I couldn't have done anything different. But I had been in charge, and three men had died. I loved the oil field, but I couldn't be a driller anymore.

My body took a couple of months to heal, and during that time I wondered where to look for a new job. I thought about going back to Mr. Ross in Overton and asking to work in the garage again.

Luckily I didn't have to do that. I was in the barbershop one day, telling Al Fisher about my situation, when another customer, an oil man, overheard and told me that the field needed engine mechanics, to keep the compressors and pumps and rig engines working. I told him that I'd worked on a lot of engines in Mr. Ross's garage, and he gave me the name of a man to contact about a job. Said I'd have to work as an apprentice for a few months at low pay, but that I'd be making good money again soon.

The man I contacted offered me a job, and I took it. Sis was thrilled that I didn't go back to the rigs, and that I worked nine-hour days instead of twelve-hour days. The pay didn't quite match what I made as a driller, but that didn't bother us. I grew to like my new job.

On a spring day in 1935 a truck from Tyler drove to the house of Al and Doris Fisher. The men in that truck carried a baby grand piano into the house, and carried the old upright back to the truck and drove away. An hour later a man from Tyler came and tuned the piano.

This all happened on a work day, a school day, but just about everybody in town wanted to see that piano and hear it played, so Al and the girls had decided ahead of time that they'd give a short concert that night after supper. Well, the word got around, and by seven o'clock there must have been two hundred people there, a couple of dozen inside the house and the others on the porch and in the yard. Because of Marty's friendship with Annie, Sis and I stood inside.

At seven o'clock Al stood on the porch and raised his hands for silence. He told us that when he first put the bowl on the table in the barbershop two and a half years earlier he didn't really believe he'd ever collect enough to buy that baby grand. He told us that the men of this community who dropped money into that bowl after their haircuts were the finest people on earth. He said that he and Doris would be the caretakers of the piano, but that the piano belonged to us, the folks who'd raised the money.

The girls had decided among themselves that Annie would play first, then Darla, then Avis. Only five or ten minutes each, just enough to let folks hear how the piano sounded.

Annie, the lively little brunette, sat at the bench, and the room hushed. She put her hands far to the left and rolled her fingers all the way up the keyboard, hands crossing. What a sound! At the top she changed from a minor key to a major key and rolled right back down. We heard "Ooooh"s and "Wow"s.

She played a little song, and Sis told me later that the song came from a picture show called *Top Hat*. Annie liked to hear the latest songs and then create her own piano versions. She finished, the crowd applauded, and Annie took a bow and went to hug Al.

Darla, the brown-haired middle child, took her seat, and she didn't need a warm-up. She flew right into "MapleLeaf Rag," to no one's surprise. Darla liked ragtime. She finished with a flourish, and that crowd went crazy—cheers and whoops and clapping. Darla grinned, went to Al and hugged him, then came to stand in front of Sis and me, next to her boyfriend Paul.

Avis was fourteen that year. Tall, calm, and confident, she made a steady contrast to her livelier sisters. She wore a yellow dress that night, and her light brown hair fell to her shoulders.

Avis took her seat. Darla turned to Paul and Marty and me and whispered, "I bet it's Schumann."

I expected something fast, loud, difficult, a show-off piece. But she began to play very softly, slowly. I doubted if the people outside could even hear it.

Darla turned and whispered, "I was wrong. It's Liszt."

Avis played only four minutes or so. The soft notes became louder, reached a peak, and then faded into softness once more. A haunting melody emerged, a repeated theme, brought forth with the right hand, then the left.

Her movements appeared so effortless. Her hands and arms seemed almost detached from her body, weaving, swimming, flowing over the keyboard with their own mind, their own mysterious knowledge.

She finished on a soft chord, held briefly with the pedal. Nobody clapped, we just stood there in silence. Finally we did clap, but Avis didn't take a bow. She went straight to Al, put her arms around his neck and whispered something in his ear, and his face glowed with pride.

One day in early 1936 I got home an hour or so late because of an emergency repair on a rig's diesel. I'd been late before, and Marty hadn't worried. I figured she'd have supper warming in the stove. But I found the house dark, and heard sobbing from her room.

She lay face down on the bed. I turned on the bedside light, put my hand on her back, and asked her what was wrong.

She sat up, still crying. "Rie and I had a fight."

"What about?"

Her voice wavered. "We were in her room talking, just normal talk, then we started arguing about something, and all of a sudden we were saying real ugly things to each other. I ran home. I've been crying ever since. I'm sorry about supper." She broke into sobs again.

I told her I'd fix supper, and to go over to Rie's and apologize, even if the argument wasn't all her fault.

She said, "I don't know what happened. I cursed her. She's my best friend that I love more than anyone except you, and I cursed her. I don't understand it."

She left the house, and I started supper. She came back in five minutes, tearless, but her face sagged. I asked her what had happened.

"Rie was getting ready to come over here. She'd been crying ever since I left. We're both sorry."

"But you still don't look happy, Sis."

"I cursed my friend. Why would you curse someone you love?"

She said little during supper and went to bed early.

Sis was quieter than usual, for the next few days, for the next few weeks. Not sullen, not withdrawn, just quieter. Well, that bothered me. Sis had always been the talker. Was she sick? A seed of worry had planted itself.

I decided to confront the worry. One April night while we washed and dried the dishes I said, "Hey, Sis, remember that walk we went on last year where you asked me if I thought you talked too much?"

She took a dish from my hand to dry. "Yeah, I remember."

"And I said you didn't, right?"

"Yeah."

"Well, you've been kinda quiet the last couple of months. I miss your happy talk."

She frowned. "I'm sorry I'm not the way you want me to be."

"It's just that you seem different, like you're worried or something."

"I'm not worried. So what if I'm different? Are *you* the same every single day?"

"Sis, I am not criticizing you. Don't be so touchy."

Her face reddened. "That *is* criticizing." I handed her a plate. It slipped from her hand and shattered on the floor.

She brought both hands to her face, then stared at me and screamed, "Why did you let go before I had it? That is *your* fault!" She ran to her room and slammed the door.

Now, we'd had accidents like that before, broken plates, broken glasses, but they'd never bothered us.

Sis apologized for her outburst the next day. I was careful what I said to her after that. The seed of worry grew and planted roots.

May rolled around. I sat on the sofa one Sunday afternoon reading the newspaper when Sis came in the front door. I glanced up at her, said "Hi," and went back to the paper. Then something clicked, and I put the paper down.

"Sis, come here a minute."

She walked out of the kitchen.

"What's that on your lips?"

She smiled and tilted her head back. "Like it? Just a little bit of lipstick. I have thin lips, and it makes me look better, don't you think?"

"Go wipe it off."

That smile left her face in a second. She didn't look at me though. She stared straight ahead and said, "Rie is beautiful. Everything is right, her lips, her eyes, her hair, everything. I'm not as pretty. My hair is mousy brown. My lips are thin. My chin is too big. I spend all afternoon trying to find just the right shade, just the right amount, and you tell me to wipe it off. Well, I'm not going to."

I found myself breathing faster. "Twelve-year old girls do not wear makeup. Go wipe it off."

She gritted her teeth. "No!"

I stood up. "Don't talk back to me, Sis."

She spit in her right hand and then drug the open palm across her lower face, smearing the lipstick on her cheek. She yelled, "There! Am I ugly enough for you now? Why do you want me not to look my best? You must *hate* me! Well, I hate you too!" She ran to the door, flung it open, and flew out of the house. She ran down the road, sobbing.

I went to the door and yelled, "Come back here!" but she kept running.

I stood there until she was out of sight. Then I sat on the couch and a great sadness came over me.

Around dusk I decided to go find her, but then heard footsteps on the porch. I yelled, "Marty?"

Rachel stood at the door. I asked if Marty was at her house. She said yes, and asked if she could sit for a minute.

When she was seated Rachel said, "When Marty came running in earlier, the thought occurred to me that you might not know what's going on."

"Going on?"

"Marty acting crazy, wild. Rie's the same way. Do you know why that is?"

"I don't have any idea, Rachel."

"Well, I'm glad I came. The girls are changing, Luke. Our babies are becoming women."

I didn't like what I heard. "Can't they become women without changing?"

Rachel laughed. "The craziness passes. They come back to their normal personalities. We need to be patient. And it's hard on us. Rie said a bad word to me today, and I almost whacked the daylights out of her, but then I remembered back when I was that age."

"Sis has been quiet lately. It bothers me."

"That talkative sweetheart will come back, I promise. Now, can Marty come stay with us for a few days?"

When I hesitated, Rachel said, "Luke, you're the sun, moon, and stars to Marty, but you're a man, and sometimes a girl needs to be around women. Let her stay with us for a while."

I nodded, and Rachel asked, "Could I get some things from her room?"

I said okay, and in a minute Rachel returned with a stack of clothes. I opened the door for her and asked her if she was going to let Marty wear lipstick. She laughed. "Of course not. They were just playing around today."

After she left I made myself supper. Somehow her words didn't make me feel any better. That seed of worry had turned into a seed of doubt. Did Sis want to live with the Erwins?

◆ ◆ ◆

The Wednesday after Marty left home was the day of the big game, London against Overton, for the district baseball championship. The schools had agreed to play at seven, under the lights, so everyone could see the game. I got there early enough to get a seat, but most people ended up standing along the first- and third-base lines.

Tim Halley, Sue and Ben's son, pitched strongly for London. Struck out most everybody. The Overton pitcher was pretty good too, but we managed to get one run in the sixth inning, the only score to that point.

I paid close attention to that game, but one time I turned to look at the crowd to my right and saw Sis and Rie and Annie together. I looked at Marty, and all of a sudden Rachel's words made sense. Her body didn't look like a little girl's body anymore. It had a shape that made me think—*woman*. Now, obviously that shape hadn't appeared in the few days since she left the house. No, it was there before, but I just hadn't noticed. Or maybe I had noticed, but had decided not to think about Sis growing up. I looked at her face, and noticed her eyes seemed different, too, more knowing, more mature.

I heard the crack of a bat and jerked my head back to the game. An Overton kid had hit a long fly to right, but the London outfielder got a good jump on the ball and made a fine running catch. We cheered.

I looked back toward Marty. Our eyes met, and she smiled and gave me a little wave with her left hand, and I waved back. Right then the strangest thing happened. In a split second, all my doubts about her love disappeared.

Gone, in a single moment. I sat there and wondered how I could have ever doubted. Sure, Marty was changing, but she hadn't stopped loving me. It seemed so obvious! Before, there were doubts. Now there were none. I didn't understand what had happened, but I felt like a heavy load had been lifted from me.

London won the game with that sixth-inning run. Tim Halley had shut 'em out. We all cheered and whooped at the last called strike.

I stood around with the crowd for a while after the game and savored the victory. I felt a tap on my shoulder and turned to look into the blue eyes of Vicky Orr. She said, "Hello, stranger."

I hadn't seen much of Vicky during her college years. I had figured she'd end up marrying a college man. I knew many men would pursue her.

"Vicky. What are you doing here? Aren't you supposed to be in college?"

She laughed. "I graduated last week. And I came here for the game, like you."

"Well, you're sure looking good these days."

"You still know how to talk to a woman, Luke. Hey, I saw Marty earlier, and she said you went from roughneck to driller to engine mechanic to overseeing other mechanics. Not out there with the slips and the tongs anymore, huh?"

I laughed. "Oh, I still remember that day. I've never laughed so hard since then. Have you?"

She shook her head and kept her eyes locked on mine.

I said, "Well, you graduated. Congratulations. What are you gonna do now?"

"Okay, here are two hints. One, I got a teaching degree. Two, I'm from Overton, but I wasn't rooting for Overton tonight. Now can you guess what I'll be doing?"

It took me a few seconds, a little longer than I think she expected, but then it clicked. "You're gonna teach here in New London?"

She laughed and nodded. "You've got a quick mind."

"Wonderful. What grade?"

"Second. And I'll be living down here. Two other teachers and I plan to rent a little house about a half mile from the school."

"That's great. But I'm a little surprised. I thought that after you went off to the big city you wouldn't want to come back here."

"Don't you remember what I told you? I'm an East Texas girl."

We stood there for a moment more, then Vicky said, "Well, I better get back to Overton. Oh, Marty said to tell you she's coming home tonight. She told me what she's been going through. I feel sorry for you, Luke. I was pure meanness at that age."

I went with Vicky to her car, and we said goodnight. Then I walked home.

Sis was sitting on the sofa. She looked up at me and said "Hi" very softly, but didn't move. I sat next to her and put my arm around her. She leaned her head against my shoulder.

She whispered, "Do you forgive me for what I said?"

"Of course I do. I'm so glad you're home. The house was so dark and quiet without you."

"Could we listen to the radio a while? Just music or something?"

I nodded, and she said, "Sit in your usual place."

My usual place was the right edge of the sofa, and hers the large chair by the fireplace. But after I sat down she picked up the little pillow from the other end of the sofa and put it in my lap, tilted it up against the sofa armrest, and lay on the sofa with her head on the pillow.

I turned on the radio, found a music station, and lowered the volume. I stroked her hair. She smiled and said, "That feels good." She was quiet for a while and then said, "Luke?"

"What, Sis?"

"Sometimes I just want to go back to the tree cave with you."

I felt a rush of memories. Walks in the woods with a little girl. "Oh, Sis, sometimes I want that too."

She held my left hand. "I remember the first time you took me there. That glorious fall day. Right before my fourth birthday. Oh, I loved that walk. Remember, we stopped in that pretty meadow and watched crows fly over, and before we left you told me to name the meadow. And I named it Crow Meadow.

"Then we got to the tree cave, and you showed me the little room you had made for me. My own room, and it had a window so I could look out. I was in heaven.

"Then we walked to the creek, and followed it down to the pond, and you climbed up into that oak tree on the bank and dropped the rope down. Then you picked me up, and I put my arms and legs around you, and you grabbed the rope and ran, and we flew out over the pond and landed on the other side of the tree. What a thrill.

"But there was another time I'll always remember too. Remember the time we went with Rie and spent the morning swinging on the rope swing? And we got so tired that after our dinner sandwiches we all crawled in the tree cave and took naps. Remember that?"

"Of course I do."

"I remember waking up after my nap to quietness, just a little breeze outside. And I could look out the little window you'd made and see the pine tree limbs moving in the wind. And all of I sudden I thought: There is no way that any girl on earth could be as lucky as me. My best friend's sleeping beside me in the room my brother made for me in his hideout, and I've just spent the morning swinging on a rope swing over a pond. I'm the luckiest girl that ever lived. That's what I thought on that day. And you know what, Luke?"

"What?"

"I still feel the same way."

A lump formed in my throat.

"I feel safe here with you, Luke. The Erwins are wonderful, but I belong with you. I feel safe here."

I kept stroking her hair, and with my other hand I wiped away a tear. "Sis, I want to tell you something that happened tonight. But first let me ask you, do you remember that day we sat in the judge's chambers, after Mom died?"

"Yes, very well."

"Remember the question the judge asked me?"

"Yeah. He asked you if you wanted to take care of me, and you said, 'Yes I do.' I'll never forget that."

"You told me later that you were worried about being a burden to me, but when I answered the judge's question, you knew I loved you and wanted you, right?"

"That's right."

"Well, something like that happened to me tonight. Because of all that's happened, I started to wonder if you still loved me. But tonight at the game, I looked at you, and you smiled and gave me a little wave, and all of a sudden all my doubts went away. All gone, in one moment. I don't understand it, but that's what happened."

She smiled. "Wow. I didn't even have to say anything, huh? Well, I don't understand that either, but I'm glad it happened. And it's true, you don't ever need to doubt my love. Even if I say things I might want to take back later."

We sat for a while longer listening to the soft music, then Marty said, "I want to go to my bed. I'm tired. I didn't sleep well on their couch."

She left for her room, but turned and said, "Luke?"

"Yeah, Sis?"

"I will wear lipstick someday." She winked.

"I know, Sis. And you'll look beautiful in lipstick. Someday."

16

Luke

Rachel had been right. The Marty I knew, the talkative sweet-heart, came back in body and spirit. I never again thought of her as a little girl, but our life together returned to a happy normalcy.

Usually we chatted at supper, after which we listened to the radio, or Marty did homework, or we read. But one night in early '37 we had a long talk after supper. Well, actually Sis did most of the talking, and I listened.

I had turned on the radio at eight for one of our favorite shows. Marty had gone to the kitchen, and I yelled, "Hey, Sis, *The Lone Ranger* is on. You coming?"

"Not tonight."

A few minutes after the show ended, she came out of the kitchen and handed me a sheet of paper. "Check this over for me, will you?"

The letters looped and swirled with an elegant precision.

Dear Miss Earhart,

I am a thirteen-year-old girl. I live in New London, in eastern Texas. Last October I rode in an airplane for the first time. It was a biplane. A man flew it to Tyler, and a crowd of us watched him do acrobatic tricks. Then he landed, and offered to take people up for two dollars each. I wanted to go, but my twenty-four-year-old brother said it cost too much. But since nobody else wanted to go, the pilot said my brother and I could go up for a dollar each. I begged my brother, and he said yes.

The plane had three seats. I sat behind the pilot, and my brother sat behind me. When we got up high, I motioned with my hand for the pilot to do a loop, and he did. It was very exciting. I don't think my brother enjoyed it as much as I did. When I looked back at him after the loop, his eyes were closed. He looked kind of pale after we landed.

There was something I didn't understand. One time I closed my eyes for a few seconds, and when I opened them the plane was leaning to one side, turning, but it didn't feel like it was leaning. My brother said it's like when you swing a bucket of water around, and the water doesn't spill out. But there was nobody swinging the plane! So I still don't understand it.

I would like to learn to be a pilot, like you. When I talk to adults about it, they don't give me much encouragement. They say it's a lot easier for boys to be pilots. Can you help me learn what I need to do to be a pilot? If you would like to write me back, I would love to hear from you. I have enclosed an envelope with our address and a stamp on it.

I read that you will be flying around the world in March, and I will be following that trip very closely, in the newspaper and on radio. I will think about you every day that you are on that trip.

Best wishes,
Marty Robertson

I handed it back. "Very nice. So you've been reading about Amelia?"

"Everything I can find. Did you know she was the first woman to fly across the Atlantic, only five years after Lindbergh? *And* the first woman to fly from Hawaii to California, two years ago?"

She sat in the chair and re-read her letter, then leaned back and gazed at the ceiling. After a while I looked up from my book. "Still thinking about Amelia?"

"Nope. My mind's wandering all over tonight. Hey, you want to hear something real sweet?"

"Sure."

"Paul finally kissed Darla. And how it happened was just so … perfect."

"Oh?"

"Yeah. They found this road, a country lane that goes through the forest to some derricks and nowhere else. Nobody drives that road on Sunday. So Darla and Paul have been taking walks down that road on Sunday afternoon. Well, last Sunday they had this conversation, and the topic was 'middles.' You know Paul's a middle child, just like Darla. Darla was complaining that being a middle is no fun, because Avis and Annie both argue with Darla but not with each other, so she has it twice as bad.

"Then Darla told him that it was not just age that made her a middle. She mentioned hair—Avis is almost a blonde, Annie's a brunette, and Darla's got brown hair—middle. Then she mentioned music. Annie's very 'now,' the latest shows, latest songs. Avis is very nineteenth-century, Germanic, Russian. Darla is ragtime and Gershwin. Middle!

"Now here's the funny part. Darla told Paul that Mrs. Gaddis had 'characterized' the girls. Annie was *allegro*, which means quick and lively, and Avis was *andante,* which means slow and graceful. Then Darla asked Paul to guess how the teacher had characterized her, and Paul said, 'Perfecto?'

"Well, Darla laughed so hard she couldn't stand up. She went off the road and fell to her knees under a pine tree. Paul laughed too. He got on his knees right next to her, and they looked at each other and stopped laughing, and Paul pulled her face to him and kissed her on the lips. Oh, that is so romantic! I want to get kissed that way the first time."

"You're a little young for that, Sis."

"Two more years. Fifteen. That's the age to get kissed. Or maybe ... fourteen."

I frowned, she giggled, and I went back to my book, but a few minutes later I noticed her smiling at me.

"All right, Sis, what are you thinking about now?"

"You."

"What about me?"

She repositioned herself in the chair. "I'm just wondering ..."

"Ask me. I got no secrets from you."

"Okay. Why don't you ever date any of the girls from around here?"

I shrugged. "Well, the single women around here are teachers. Been to college. I doubt if they'd want to date a high-school dropout with grease under his fingernails."

She shook her head. "Not a good answer. There's no grease under your fingernails when you go out with the Kilgore women. And forget that 'dropout' stuff. I know there are girls around here who'd like to go out with you."

"Oh? And just who would those ladies be?"

"Well, Vicky, for one. She still likes you. We talk now and then. Her roommate's my English teacher, and Vicky comes by the high school sometimes after her school lets out. I can tell from what Vicky says that she'd love to go out with you."

"I like Vicky. I just don't think I'm her type. She's pretty and smart both. She could date anybody, people with a lot more money and brains. I'm surprised she's not married."

Marty shook her head and sighed.

"What's the problem with the Kilgore ladies?" I asked. "There's nurse Judy, and Leona, and Carol, and—"

"I don't like them. You come home smelling like a lit cigarette. I'll bet they drink whiskey too."

A silent moment, then Marty stretched her arms above her head and said, "You asked earlier who were the girls who liked you. I said Vicky. That's one. You want to hear another one?"

"Nothing to lose, Sis. Go ahead."

"There's a difference. Other people know that Vicky likes you. But this one, it's kind of a secret. Not too many people know." She smiled.

"Well, how long do I have to wait?"

She said the word softly. "Avis."

"Little Avis Fisher? Oh, come on, Marty. What is she, sixteen? I'm eight years older than her. You don't know what you're talking about."

She settled back in the chair with a knowing smile. "Mom and Dad were twelve years apart. And Avis'll be seventeen in three months. That's not little."

"All right, Miss know-it-all, and just what makes you think Avis Fisher is so fond of me?"

Marty sat up. "It was the night of the blowout, and I didn't remember it 'til later 'cause I was so upset myself. I had gone to the Erwins's, worried about you, and learned about the well blowout. But we didn't know if it was your well, and we had to wait about an hour to find out. What a horrible hour. Anyway, I remember Annie being there at first, and she must have gone home and told the rest of the family. Annie never came back, but Avis did. She sat in a corner of the living room with her head bowed, and she put her hands together and leaned her head on her hands. And when we finally got the call that you were all right, she cried for joy."

"Well, there's a difference between concern and wanting to date somebody, I think."

"Luke, I'm over at that house a lot. She asks about you. Trust me. I'm only thirteen, but I can see things."

I grinned and shook my head. "Al Fisher would have me arrested if I asked Avis for a date."

Marty stood. "Well, I'm going to bed. You can think what you wish. But let me warn you about something. Avis has a way of getting what she wants."

"What do you mean?"

"She got a new piano, didn't she?"

17

Luke

I'll never forget the last haircut I ever got from Al Fisher. Everything seemed so normal then, so steady. That world seems very far away now.

I'm pretty sure it was a Saturday morning. There were a few other fellows in the shop, and I had to wait a few minutes for my haircut, but when I sat down in the chair I was the one to speak first. "Tell me about the audition, Al. Marty told me it didn't go quite the way you expected."

Al took comb and scissors in hand and began his work. "Nope. But we're all real happy with how it turned out. Avis won't be so far away. I never liked that idea of her in Chicago."

"Start at the beginning. Marty told me a little, but I want to hear it from you."

"Sure. Last month Avis was offered the chance to audition for Mr. Mowinckel, a very famous piano teacher at the University of Chicago. Mr. Mowinckel picks a few students every year to begin study with him and at the same time to start college at the university. At the end of four years those students have both a college degree and a head start toward a career as a concert pianist. And here's the nice part: Mr. Mowinckel is very rich—he's a former concert pianist and made a lot of money. If he picks you to study with him, he pays all the cost of your education for all four years. And a lot of his students have gone on to be concert pianists, making a lot of money, thirty thousand, fifty thousand a year, some of 'em.

"You can imagine it's very competitive to get to be one of his students. In fact, to even audition with him you have to have almost straight As in school and have to have won a big piano competition. Well, Avis's grades qualify, and she won that regional competition in Dallas two years ago, so she applied to audition and was accepted.

"Mr. Mowinckel goes around the country by train for the auditions so the kids don't have to travel too far. He came to Dallas two weeks ago, and that's where Avis had the audition. She and I took the train up.

"We went to this big hotel and took the elevator to the top floor. Mr. Mowinckel had rented a suite with several rooms. He met us and took us into this big room where there was a huge concert grand piano. He was a tall man, with thick gray hair a little too long for my liking. He had a deep clear voice and a sort of military bearing, like he was used to giving orders.

He told me to wait in another room while Avis did the audition. Well, I turned around to do as he said, and I heard Avis say, 'I'd like my father to be here, please.'

"He looked a little surprised, then he frowned and said, a bit loudly, 'No. Only the student and I are in the room for the auditions.' And Avis just stood there with the same polite little smile on her face, and she said again, 'I'd like my father to be here, please.'

"He looked like he was gonna say something more, but they just ended up looking at each other for a few seconds. Then he said, 'All right, Miss Fisher,' and pointed me to a chair in the corner of the room. Avis smiled and said, 'Thank you, sir.'

"The first part of the audition, the student plays a piece of their choice, from memory, no more than ten minutes long. Avis played a movement from a Schubert sonata, and it sounded fine to me, and I could see that Mr. Mowinckel even smiled a little bit as she was playing. And he said, 'Very nice,' after she finished.

"Then he reached over to a table and picked up a piece of sheet music, and he said, 'You won't have seen this before. I wrote it myself. This is the only copy that exists. I'd like you to look at it for as long as you want, then keep it in front of you and play it. I'll turn the pages for you. Just nod.'

"Well, it was only four pages, one folded sheet. She looked at the first three pages for about thirty seconds each, but then she spent a long time, maybe two minutes, on the fourth page. Then she started playing.

"She looked very confident as her fingers flew over the keys, and I saw Mr. Mowinckel's eyes getting a little bigger, and there was a smile on his face. It was a pretty piece, and I could tell he liked what she was doing with it.

"Then came the fourth page, and it sounded to me like it was getting even stronger, a beautiful, inventive harmony, and then I noticed that the man wasn't smiling anymore. In fact, he had a frown. She finished with a flourish, and it was all I could do to keep from clapping, but then Mr. Mowinckel said, 'That is not what is written.' And Avis looked up at him, and she had the same little polite smile, and she said, 'I was trying to bring out the main theme better.'

"Well, that man's face turned as red as a beet, and he was perfectly quiet, he just kept looking at Avis, and she looked right back at him. Finally he said, 'Thank you for coming,' and showed us to the elevator.

"She was pretty quiet on the train ride back. I didn't say much either, I figured she would talk when she was ready. We were almost back to Overton when out of the blue she said, 'What I did was ugly and selfish. As soon as I get home I'll write him a letter of apology. But ...'

"She drew out the word 'But' and just left it hanging.

"I said, 'But what?'

"She turned to me. 'I need to tell you something, Daddy. On the train ride to Dallas yesterday I decided I don't want to be a concert pianist.'

"That was a shock. I said, 'Really?'

"She nodded. 'Remember the contest in San Antonio, and the boy that won?'

"'Sure.'

"'He'll be a good concert pianist. He had a flair, a need to please, to show off, to draw attention to himself, his technique, his skill. He *ruled* that piano! Following him on the program was very hard for me. But now I know I don't want to make music like that. I want to teach others. I want to go to the University of Texas and study music. But, since we'd already made the trip, I decided to go through with the audition. So when we got to Mr. Mowinckel's penthouse, I knew right away what kind of person he was. I could never have worked with him. He was a snob. You could tell from all the things in that room. Now, his little bagatelle was a very nice piece, but ...'

"She left that last word hanging again. I said, 'But what?'

"'But it needed fixing. He had a good main theme, but he kind of frittered it away near the end. The piece kind of ... turned purple. He needed to raise it up a key, restate the main theme, reharmonize. I did that. I colored it yellow. But ...'

"Once again the last word floated in the air. I said, 'But what?'

"She frowned. 'But what I did was wrong. Maybe even cruel. I'll apologize, but I never should have done it. I'm a selfish person. I need fixing, just like Mr. Mowinckel's little bagatelle.'

"So, Luke, Avis will go to the University. Four-hour train ride down to Austin. That's close. I don't want my girls to ever be too far away."

18

Luke

I still remember the day of the week, Tuesday, and I remember everything Sis talked about that morning at breakfast. Many, many times I've thought about that conversation, how normal it seemed at first, and how a few words turned routine happiness into fear.

I fixed us oatmeal that morning. Sis came to the table, handed me a piece of paper, and asked how I'd pronounce the word she had written. I looked at the paper, saw "Kreisleriana," and pronounced it as best I could. Told her I'd never seen the word before.

She said, "It's German. Avis pronounced it for me, but I keep forgetting how to say it. I really want to take a foreign language. But I think I'd rather learn French. I heard somebody talking French on the radio one time, and it sounded so smooth, kind of romantic."

Sis started on her oatmeal, and I looked at her paper again. "What's Avis's word mean?"

"Don't know. All I know is it's the name of one of the pieces Avis is gonna play on Saturday. But her teacher almost didn't let her put that piece in her program."

"Why not?"

"'Cause it's real hard, real advanced. Avis chose it, but the teacher said no at first. Then Avis told the teacher to give her a month, and if she couldn't play it well enough after a month, she'd leave it out of her concert. Well, two weeks ago she played it for the teacher, and the teacher said okay."

"Why'd she choose such a hard one for her senior recital? She knows so many pieces already."

Marty smiled. "Annie told me the reason. It's because a woman named Clara played it a long time ago, back in the last century. Avis read the biography of that lady, and now she wants to play everything Clara did.

"Clara was such a good pianist that this composer, Mr. Schumann, got interested in her and pursued her. He's the one who wrote that piece Avis is gonna play. They finally married, but Avis says the pieces he wrote after they married weren't as good as the ones he wrote before, so she's not sure Clara should've married him.

"Oh, Avis got her recital dress last week. It's yellow, her favorite color. You're planning to go hear her on Saturday, aren't you?"

"Sure am."

Sis finished off her oatmeal, then said, "I just hope it's warm again Saturday, like three days ago. I thought spring had come, but then Monday it turned cold again, and we had to wear coats. You know what? We even had to keep our coats on in class yesterday."

"Oh, why?"

"Teacher had to open the windows. She said the radiators didn't work. Some of the kids felt sick. Our eyes got teary."

Her words registered, and when they did, all else left my mind except for the memory of two men, face down on a drilling rig floor, seen through my wet eyes.

"Sis, did you say tears came in your eyes?"

"A little, yeah. They went away after she opened the windows."

"Did the teacher say what was wrong with the radiators?"

"The flames weren't steady. They kept going up and down."

I raised my voice. "What flames? What are you talking about?"

"The radiators have these burners. That's what heats them up."

I stared at her. My mouth must have dropped open because Sis said, "You look funny."

Radiators. Steam flowing inside the pipes heats the air around the pipes. But the steam comes from somewhere, from a boiler. The radiators themselves don't make steam. Her words made no sense.

I said, "I want to go to school with you. I want you to show me the radiators."

"Good. You'll get to meet Miss Penrose. She's one of Vicky's roommates."

Sis started to clear the table, but I told her to forget the dishes, that I wanted us to leave right away, so I'd have some time at the school before classes started.

Sis introduced me to her English teacher, Penny Penrose, and we went to the radiator at the side of the room. I asked Penny about the problem that had occurred the day before, and she said the gas pressure wasn't steady, and the burners didn't work right. But she said that after school a man from the radiator company had come and made an adjustment, and that things were normal today.

I knelt, and through a little access hole I could see blue flames about an inch high above the dozen or so orifices in the burner unit. I asked Penny if that type of radiator was in every classroom, and she said yes. I asked if Monday was the first time she'd had the problem, and she said no, they'd been having problems ever since the school started using a different gas company a few weeks earlier.

I didn't have a reason to stay any longer, so I thanked the teacher, said good-bye to Marty, and drove to work. On that drive and all during the day I kept thinking, Why individual heaters? For a one-room school, sure, maybe even for three or four rooms. But for a school London's size, how much more efficient to generate the steam in a boiler and pipe it to each classroom. Pipe steam over the school, not gas. One large burner, not fifty or sixty small ones. A handful of gas pipe fittings, not a hundred. So why had they done it?

I remembered something else Penny had said, about a different gas company. Why a different company? What would that have to do with the radiator burners acting up?

After supper that night I left Sis to her homework and walked to the school. I stood facing the front steps and looked at the white brick building, the junior-senior high school of one of the wealthiest rural school districts in the country. Seven producing oil wells on campus. Royalty income. While the rest of the country was trying to crawl out of a Depression, here was a school district with no shortage of money. So why the odd, probably dangerous, method of heating the building?

I walked down the slope to the back of the school, behind the auditorium where Avis would give her recital on Saturday. The auditorium was the middle wing of an *E*. The front of the school was the long part of the *E*, and the north and south wings were the top and bottom of the *E*. Unlike the front, the wings had two stories, because of the land's downward slope from front to back.

On the side of the south wing I found what I sought. A two-inch pipe rose vertically from the ground, atop it a standard gas regulator. From the regulator a smaller horizontal pipe entered a hole in the wall of the school, below the level of the floor of the classrooms.

A light-colored earth surrounded the pipe, and a three-foot-wide strip of light-colored soil led away from the building. The earth had been turned. A trench had been dug there, not long before.

I followed the strip south, away from the school, for a quarter-mile. There the strip ended. Then I knew that the new pipe had been connected to an older pipe that had been buried much earlier.

To the northeast, past the school, a gas flare spread its orange glow. I could see other flares in the distance. A memory came back to me.

A few years earlier Sis and I had taken a walk after supper on a pleasant night after the first cool front of the fall. On that walk Sis had asked me why there were so many gas flares in the oil field. "Doesn't it just waste the gas?" she had asked.

I remembered telling her it's cheaper to flare gas than to store it, since the gas doesn't have much value after the gasoline and butane and propane have been taken out of it. That low-value gas is called residue gas.

Then Sis asked if you could use the gas to heat houses, and I told her yes, some people in the oil camps did use the residue gas to heat their houses. Some of the churches did too. The oil companies didn't mind.

I looked back at the school, then at the trench, then at the flare, and I knew what had been done: *The school gas supply had been hooked to a residue gas line.*

Why? To save money? I could imagine a desperately poor school district doing something like that. But a wealthy district?

And how reliable was the supply? What about pressure variations? What about the gas itself, its content?

Ben Halley would know. A school board member, a respected community leader. And a member of our church. I knew I could count on Ben to give me the truth.

A few minutes later I knocked on his door. Sue, the petite red-head, appeared. "How nice to see you, Luke. Come in." Her soft voice tended to fade, but her smile was genuine.

"Thank you, Sue. Is Ben here?"

"No, he's in Overton at the bank tonight, meeting with some investors. Can you come back tomorrow?"

Tomorrow—Wednesday. I had a date with Judy. A new dance hall had opened.

"How about if I come by Thursday after supper?"

"That'll be fine. We'll be looking for you."

I wondered if she knew anything. "Sue, did Ben say anything about a different gas supply for the school recently?"

She smiled again. "Oh, yes. The board's real happy about that. They're saving the school a lot of money."

"Did Ben ever say anything about residue gas?"

"No … I don't remember hearing that …"

I would learn no more that night. "Thanks, Sue. Tell Ben I'll see him Thursday. Say, has Tim picked a college yet?"

She beamed with pride. "No, but Texas, TCU, and SMU have all offered him full baseball scholarships."

We said goodnight, and I started home. I thought of Ben Halley. A banker, a careful man, a smart man. His only son a student at the school. Surely the board wouldn't allow the school district to do anything to put the school in danger. They had to know what they were doing. Sue's soft voice had somehow eased my worries.

A gentle breeze carried the song of a piano, and I decided to make a detour. When I neared the Fisher house I saw, through the open front window, Avis at the keyboard. And, oh, the melody that came through that window. I stood still and drank it in.

She finished the piece, and I waited a minute, hoping to hear more. I turned back to the road, then heard a voice. "Hi, Luke."

She stood on the front porch, and the door was closed behind her.

I waved. "Hi, Avis. That was sure pretty."

She raised her right hand and motioned with her long fingers. "Come here, Luke, I can't hear you!"

I went to the porch and stepped up. "I said, that was sure pretty. I started listening to you , and I sort of couldn't move."

"What a sweet thing to say."

"What was that piece you played? Was that Schumann? Are you going to play that piece Saturday?"

"It's called a barcarolle, by Rubinstein, not Schumann. Yes, I'll play it Saturday. Are you coming?"

"Bark-a-what?"

She laughed, spelled it for me, and said something about alternating strong and weak beats. I told her that yes, I would be there Saturday.

She said, "Come on in, I'll play it for you again right now."

"Oh, you don't need to do that, Avis."

She opened the door and motioned me in. "I need the practice." She sat on the bench and pointed to the right. "Stand there."

She played, and her eyes went from the keyboard, to me, back to the keyboard, back to me. Her arms and hands made their own journey, closing, then separating, closing, separating.

She finished, and I told her I didn't understand how a human being could make music that beautiful. I asked her how her fingers knew where to go. She laughed and said it was a good question, and she didn't know the answer herself.

She pushed back the bench. "Let's go out on the porch." I followed her out, and she told me to close the door behind me.

She stood close and smiled but didn't say anything. Finally I said, "I hear you're going to the University of Texas. My dad told me Austin's a pretty town."

"Yes … but I don't leave until September, and I'll be home for Thanksgiving and Christmas."

Even in the fading light her hazel eyes seemed to sparkle. All of a sudden it seemed I was not talking with a girl but with a beautiful woman. I remembered Marty's words, "Avis has a way of getting what she wants."

Then she said, "And you know what I think would be fun? I want you and Marty to drive down and see me some weekend. I can show you the town."

I nodded, unsure how to reply. She was just seventeen, but …

She said, "Bring Annie. She can talk to Marty while you and I talk."

I smiled. "I think that's a real nice idea."

We stood in silence. Her smile never wavered, and her eyes never left mine.

Finally I said, "Goodnight. Thanks for playing that piece."

"I'll be looking for you Saturday."

I nodded, turned and walked off the front porch. I waved to her from the driveway, and she waved back. I walked fifty feet down the road, turned, and saw that she hadn't moved. I waved, and she echoed.

In bed that night, Avis's melody came alive again in my mind, but incompletely. Parts, segments, small melodies within a larger one. I stayed awake a long time trying to put those parts together. I couldn't do it. But on Saturday I would hear it again, and the parts would become whole.

I decided that Sis and I would leave early Saturday to get seats near the front of the auditorium.

But other thoughts intruded on Avis and her melody as I waited for sleep. Why the individual heaters? Why the change to residue gas? I thought of Sue Halley and her soft, gentle voice that seemed to ease my worries. Whatever had transpired, the school board had approved. Ben Halley and the others, all knowledgeable men, most of whom had children in the school. They would never approve of anything that would put the school at risk.

◆ ◆ ◆

Judy was a drinker, like Carol and Leona. I always ended up with a drinker. I'd been out with a couple of "nice" girls, but those women had seemed bland and predictable. I liked the women who laughed and knew how to make me laugh, and who weren't afraid to let their hair down and have a good time.

Judy was a nurse at a Kilgore hospital, a dark-haired little fireball who never wanted the nights to end.

I picked her up Wednesday around eight, and she told me how to get to the new honky-tonk on the Gladewater-Longview highway. We drove into the parking lot and saw the sign: Wednesday Nights—No Cover Charge. Judy told me I could buy her more setups with the money I saved. She asked if I'd brought our usual pint, and I said yes.

The room was packed, the smoke thick, the band revved up. We danced now and then but spent most of the night at our table, drinking and listening to the high song of the fiddle, the twang of a steel guitar, and the back beat of drums.

Around eleven Judy poured the last of the rum into her cola and put her hand on my cheek. "You having a good time, handsome?"

"Sure am. Good music, good company."

"Me too, Luke. But our rum's all gone." She puckered her lips in a little pout.

"Yeah, but this is a work night, hon."

She smiled. "Yeah, I knew you'd say that. You're so … responsible. But I've got a surprise for you, big boy." She opened her purse and pulled out a bottle of rum.

"A whole pint? Oh, come on, Judy."

"Now don't get excited. We're not gonna drink the whole thing.

But it's too early to go. I love that band. We'll have one more drink. Now get us some setups. How about a little sandwich to go with them?"

I'm not sure what time we finally left. I looked at my watch once, but couldn't focus on the hands.

I had to drag Judy away from that table. She whined that there was still an inch left in the bottle, and that I was a meanie for not letting her drink it. We strolled out into the cool night air, arm in arm for support. I breathed deeply, hoping to clear my head.

I drove her home, thankful that the roads were nearly empty. A half-hour later I pulled into my driveway and stepped from the car. I started toward the front porch, then leaned over and vomited a bunch of rum and cola and whatever else onto the dirt. I heaved for a couple of minutes, then staggered into the house and fell on my bed. I managed to kick off my shoes. I lay on the bed in the dark and told myself: Never again. No more Judy. Never, ever again.

I waited for the room to stop moving. Then I saw Sis in the doorway in her nightgown, her face shadowed. She said, "You're drunk," then left my sight.

◆ ◆ ◆

I woke with a headache to a quiet house, and realized from the light that I had overslept. I looked at the clock and knew that Sis had made her own breakfast and left for school.

The headache stayed all morning, but after the dinner sandwich I felt my life coming back. I worked with another fellow doing routine maintenance on a set of diesel pumpers south of Kilgore.

In mid-afternoon we finished up our work and were ready to restart the engines when we heard a strange noise, a deep, loud thud that shook the ground. We glanced at each other, then put down our tools and walked out beyond the pumps to the open area next to the road. I thought, Well blowout, and looked for black smoke. Then I saw my partner point to the south. I followed his gaze and saw, low over the pine trees, a whitish cloud. We stared at it for a minute. White smoke? A forest fire? But ... the thud?

Thud. Explosion. White. Something white exploded. White what? White ... brick.

I screamed out, "What time is it?" I shoved my hand into my pocket and brought out the watch. Nineteen minutes after three. Junior high still in session.

I ran for my car, screaming, "No! No! No!"

19

Luke

Down the dirt road, over the wooden bridges, churning up the red dust. Finally, pavement. Sharp left turn, tires squealing, accelerator pedal pressed to the floor. Highway 42, the road toward the white cloud, toward home, toward her school. My heart pounded, and a big pit seemed to open underneath me, a pit of dread. Oh, that pit had a pull, Russ! But I tried to stay above it.

The refinery, I told myself. An explosion at the little refinery north of town. A big butane tank, maybe. Sitting right next to a white brick office building. The tank blew and pulverized the building. That's the cloud.

I passed that refinery a minute later, and the cloud loomed ahead, billowing, drifting. The pit widened and deepened, and I fought to keep from falling.

I drove over the final hill and saw, through a haze of white dust, a pile of rubble. Behind the rubble were buildings I recognized, and I knew then that the pile of rubble had been classrooms a few minutes earlier.

But I saw something else. Children standing, walking, kneeling.

There were survivors! I drove close, braked to a stop, and jumped from the car. I ran to every girl: those standing, those sitting, those lying still on the ground. I looked at every face. She wasn't among them.

A man yelled, "Mary! Mary!" and tore at the rubble with his bare hands. A woman walked in a tight circle, bowing, chanting, her hands clasped in front of her. The wail of a siren grew louder.

The pit hadn't swallowed me yet. If some had survived, others had too. But there were no sounds, no cries, from the rubble. The words I heard came from behind me, from the growing crowd of adults, and the words were "God," "Jesus" and "mercy," and the voices were high-pitched with fear, horror, disbelief.

I saw a woman standing near the southeast wing, her arms around a dark-haired girl. I ran toward them. "Rie! Rachel!"

Rachel reached out for me. "Luke. My darling is safe! Have you seen Neil?"

I lowered my face to Rie's wide and vacant eyes. "Rie, were you in class with Marty?"

She stared right through me. I put my face closer. "Rie, look at me. Do you know what Marty was wearing?"

Rachel pulled her away. "Leave Rie alone. She's too shocked to talk. Why don't you know what Marty was wearing?"

"Shut up, Rachel! Let me talk to her!"

She swung her right arm, and her open hand cracked across my face. But right away she said, "I'm sorry. I'm sorry. Luke, find Neil. Find Marty. I've got to get Rie out of here. Oh, God, please save my little boy!"

My face stung from her slap. I watched her pull Rie through the growing crowd. An ambulance had stopped, and the men began loading children, many covered with blood. I saw sheets on the ground, sheets covering forms, bodies.

I saw men on top of the rubble. Rescue. I would have to join them. But not right away.

Why don't you know what Marty was wearing? Only one way to find out. My car was useless. Rescue vehicles, oil workers, parents swarmed over the road.

I began to run. I needed something to keep me above the pit. An idea, a rope. I found one. Maybe Marty had not felt well at school and had come home at noon.

That rope snapped like a thin thread. Marty was never sick. I grabbed a new rope, one toughened by logic. Like Rie, Marty had survived, but had run home immediately. Yes, that's what she would do. She would be afraid, and she would run to where she felt safe. She was there now, waiting for me, and I would pick her up and hold her and rock her and comfort her.

I bounded onto the porch and flung open the door. I shouted her name. I darted from room to room. The rope dissolved in my hands. But I had to stay above the pit. I needed to join the rescue effort.

I went to her room, pulled the middle drawer from the dresser, and emptied it on her bed. She had five dresses. But there was no pattern, no certain dress on a certain day. Which one was missing? I stared at them. Dark blue with light yellow collar. Dark brown and deep red with pink collar. White floral with orange bow at the top. Light blue with white stripes and white belt. I closed my eyes and tried to imagine her leaving the house each day, or cooking, or sitting in the swing waiting for me, or listening to the radio, or doing her homework.

I remembered a blue dress with tiny white flowers. I ran from the house and heard, from the south, a symphony of sirens.

I stopped at my car for gloves and walked toward the rubble pile. From behind, a woman's voice. "Luke!"

Vicky ran up and grabbed my arm. "Marty?"

"Will you look for her, Vicky?"

"Yes, of course."

"She had on a blue dress with white flowers and a white collar. If you find her, come get me. I'll be out here all night."

"I remember the dress. I'll start right now." She started to turn away, but I took her arm.

"Vicky, do you know where her last class was? She said you sometimes came to the high school after your school let out."

"Seventh-grade English. Penny's class."

I grabbed at another rope. "Was Rie Erwin in that class?"

"No."

"Have you seen Penny?"

Her voice broke. "I can't find her."

"I got to go help the men, Vicky."

She patted my arm and turned toward the ambulances.

Penny's class. On the west side of the building, near the front. Not the back, where parts of the building still stood. The front—crumbled, devastated.

I walked to the edge of the rubble and found a man who appeared to be giving orders. I told him that I could lift, and asked him to tell me what to do.

Chain man, that's what they called me that night. Under the glow of huge klieg lights brought in from the oil field I hooked the chains around the big chunks of concrete and steel so the truck-mounted winches could pull them away. I didn't start out with that job. I watched another man struggle with the chains until I got irritated and pushed him aside and said I'd do it. He didn't argue.

We did find children alive under the rubble, in those early hours of the night. We heard cries, and we pulled and dug and lifted and uncovered children and saved them. We worked as a team, the other men and I. We gave orders, we took orders. We cautioned, we advised, we motioned for help. Our voices had an urgency in those early hours. We'd hear things like, "Hurry men, over here. I hear crying. Come on, lift that beam. Watch that edge. More lifters over here. To the right, to the right. Now up. There she is! She's breathing. Use crowbars, get that block off her leg. We're coming, honey!"

I listened for the cries of girls. Each cry was a rope that held me a while longer.

The cries went away after midnight, and left only the hiss of acetylene torches, the ring of chains against concrete, and the growls of winch motors.

We knew we were beaten when the cries went away. We knew we weren't rescuing anymore. We all began to sound the same. Same flat, defeated tones.

"What's that, you found a shoe with a foot still in it? Put it in the sheet. You, with the torch. Cut that beam, pull away that water pipe. That a body there? No, just an arm. Put it in the sheet. Keep going, men. Dawn's a long way off. Chain man, over here. Drag this chunk away."

Strength flowed out of my body like blood from a wound. An hour or so before dawn I heard a man to my right say, "Looks like another teacher."

I followed his gaze and saw blonde hair and a still face covered with mortar dust. I crawled to the body. I wiped dust from the eyes and recognized the face of Penny Penrose. Seventh-grade English. I leaned forward on my hands. "I can't do it anymore."

A voice boomed from my left. "You, chain man! Take a break. Go get coffee and a sandwich. That's an order!"

I rose and staggered out of the rubble. I found the coffee buckets, and a woman poured me a cup and gave me a ham sandwich. I sat on the ground and drank and ate. Sirens howled as one ambulance after another came for its cargo and departed.

I stood, put on my gloves, and walked to where men were loading dump trucks with broken concrete to be hauled away. I started to pick up concrete chunks and throw them into the back of a truck. I looked for the heaviest pieces. I felt rain drops on my face.

After a few minutes I became aware of a person, a woman, standing between my dump truck and another one. At first I thought: What is she doing out here? It's raining. She should be back with the women.

Then a horror crept over me. I couldn't look at that woman again. I wanted her to leave. I picked up the concrete chunks and tossed them.

I heard her say the word "Luke," but I didn't look at her. Then she said, "You need to come to Overton with me."

I searched for the biggest piece of concrete. I picked up the jagged block and heaved it, and it crashed into the truck bed with a boom like thunder.

She said, "Come now, Luke."

I turned to her and cursed her with the vilest words I knew. I thought: She's a decent woman. She'll be shocked to hear those words. She'll turn and run away, sobbing.

But she didn't run away. She moved closer and said, "I'll drive. Come to Overton with me, Luke."

I jabbed a finger toward her and yelled, "Leave! Now! You're not even supposed to be out here! This is men only! This is rescue! Get back with the women where you belong! Make coffee! Make sandwiches! We gotta eat! Now, leave!"

She just stood there in the rain, and watched me toss more concrete into the dump truck.

I searched for another rope, but all the ropes were gone. I finally looked at Vicky and said, "Where's your car?"

We drove the four miles to Overton. We didn't say a word to each other. All I heard was the flip-flop of windshield wipers, and now and then a siren.

Vicky pulled to a stop behind a line of cars parked on the street. Up ahead was a building with a light above the door, and below the light was a sign: American Legion Hall.

I didn't want to leave the car, but Vicky came around and opened my door and took my hand. I held her hand, and we walked toward the building.

A sound came from that building, a sound beyond describing. Tones, high and low, all mixed together, a chorus from a nightmare. Women crying, wailing, each in a different pitch, a different voice.

Vicky led the way inside. On the tables were sheets, and under the sheets forms that gave horrible shape to the sheets.

Vicky walked to a back wall, stopped, and turned to me. To my right, sticking out from beneath a sheet, was a boy's shoe. I looked down to my left, and saw black shoes, familiar shoes, and two pale legs, and the hem of a blue dress. I saw three small white flowers against the blue. My world fell away and shattered, like a dish shatters on a hard floor. The pit swallowed me.

I knelt and pulled away the sheet. Through her sobs Vicky told me that Marty's face was fine, that she looked like she was sleeping, that something heavy had fallen on her and crushed the life out of her.

I looked at Vicky. "It didn't hurt her?"

"She died right away, Luke. Went straight to heaven."

I don't have any idea how long I knelt there, but Vicky stayed. Eventually I heard a voice above me. "Sir?"

I raised my head. A woman, dressed in white, carried a clipboard. "Is that your daughter, sir?"

I stood. She wore dark-rimmed glasses. Her black hair was pulled back, and her face was flat, emotionless. Her bloodshot eyes focused on my lower face. She repeated her question.

My brain had pretty much shut down, but I finally figured out what she was asking. "She's my sister."

"I'm very sorry," she said to my mouth. "Do her parents know?"

"They died. I'm her guardian."

"I'm so sorry. Could I get her name from you?"

I took a deep breath and let it out. "Her name is Martha Lee Robertson."

She wrote, and without looking up asked, "Age?"

"Thirteen."

The tip of her pencil clicked on the paper.

"Grade?"

"Seventh."

"Thank you, sir. I need to leave. Lots more to talk to." She turned and walked away.

Behind me a man sobbed, and I thought, I should be crying like that man, but I can't.

I walked to the man. He sat in a folding chair with his head in his hands. When I got near, he raised up, and I saw the round face of my barber Al. He recognized me and stood.

"Did your little Marty die, Luke?"

I stared at him and shook my head, but then I nodded.

His voice wavered in a low pitch. "Is she all together?"

I didn't know what he meant, but then I did. I breathed harder, and nodded.

Then Al grabbed me by the shoulders and said loudly, "Then you're a very lucky man. Your Marty's all together."

My breath came faster. I whispered a word. "Avis?"

The lady in white marched up to Al, her eyes narrowed. "Sir, please lower your voice. There are many grieving parents here."

But Al Fisher raised his face and yelled, "My darlings are in pieces!"

"Somebody stop him!" shouted a man from across the room. Women screamed in tones of fresh horror.

The lady in white gritted her teeth and barked, "You be quiet!"

Men converged on Al, and their hands reached out for him, but the words poured forth. "My darlings are in pieces! All three! They can't find all the pieces!"

The men drug him away, to a kitchen in the back of the hall. I watched for a second, then ran for the door, stumbled down the steps, fell to my hands and knees, and vomited into the wet grass. Vicky came and knelt beside me, and when I was finished she pulled my head to her breast and stroked my hair and whispered, "I want to comfort you."

Through the open door we could still hear Al's shouts. "Nobody can put them back together! Why have you sent us to hell? What have we done? Oh, what have we done?" The sky had turned gray with the dawn, and the rain fell and formed pools in the red earth.

◆ ◆ ◆

The next thing I remembered was a hand on my arm, waking me out of a dreamless sleep. I was on my couch, and Vicky was kneeling beside me.

She said, "Luke, I'm sorry to wake you, but they've got to plan a lot of funerals for tomorrow. They need some decisions." Her voice was weak, her eyes red.

I sat up and put my hand to my face and remembered a form under a sheet. I wished I hadn't woken up. Finally I said, "What's that smell?"

"I made dinner for you. You have to eat."

I looked out the window. "What time is it?"

"Two o'clock. You've been asleep since eight. Luke, I need to get back to the church. The funeral will be at eleven-fifteen tomorrow, is that all right?"

"What funeral?"

She stared at me, and I finally nodded.

She said, "I understand. Now, do you want her buried in the dress she's wearing, or another one?"

What does it matter, I thought. "The same."

"Burial at Pleasant Hill, where your mother is?"

I nodded.

"For the funeral, is there any music you want, any hymn, something Marty liked a lot?"

For some reason I felt an anger. I stood up and said, "I don't want any music at the service."

Vicky stood and said, "Don't say that, Luke. She loved music. She loved to sing. Please, please don't say that."

I said, "If it's so all-fired important, you pick a hymn. I'm too tired to think."

"I will. I know a hymn she liked. I need to go to the church now. Eat your dinner. You need to be strong for tomorrow. I'll come by later."

She patted my arm and left the house. I lay back down on the couch and found myself wondering what time Sis would be home.

◆ ◆ ◆

I remember the funeral itself, Saturday morning, ten minutes, fifteen minutes, I can't remember. Many others were waiting. Vicky sat with me. I was glad to have someone to sit with me. I remember the Erwins not being there, and I asked Vicky why, and she said that Neil had died from his injuries, and that his funeral was at the same time in the Baptist church. I didn't recognize the pastor, and Vicky told me that they brought in preachers from other towns, some for the church services, some for the graveside services. I don't remember a single word that pastor said at Marty's funeral. I do remember the hymn Vicky chose, "Fairest Lord Jesus."

I remember the lines of cars that snaked down the road from Old London to Pleasant Hill. I remember the mounds of red-orange earth, row after row. I remember standing with Vicky at the grave, and hearing two pastors speak. One of them was at a grave about twenty feet away, and he had a loud voice. My preacher's voice sounded weak, shallow. I found myself getting angry at him, just like I got angry at Daddy's funeral. Why couldn't he talk loud, with conviction, like the man at the other grave? My baby sister deserved better.

I remember Vicky touching my arm as we walked back toward the car. She pointed, and we turned in that direction. Rachel and Tom and Rie were walking from a grave toward the gate. I called to them, and Rachel ran to me and fell into my arms. "Oh, Luke, you know I loved her like a daughter, don't you? I'm so sorry we missed her funeral. But I had to bury my little boy." I held Rachel while she sobbed, and Vicky went to hug Rie. Tom stood alone, his head bowed.

I paced a lot in the days after the funeral. To Sis's room, then back to the kitchen, over and over. Sometimes at night I'd leave the house and walk up and down the street until dawn, then go home and try to sleep.

In my naps I had a dream, the same one, over and over. Marty stood in front of me, and I would say to her "Sis, I need to tell you something!" She would smile, and I would reach for her, but she'd be just outside my grasp. I would strain to touch her, but touch only air.

After five days I found a new routine. I'd get up, eat something, then walk the four and a half miles to Sis's grave, rest for an hour, then go back home. I'd do the same thing after dinner. This helped me kill the daylight hours.

My boss came by and told me I should come back to work. I had no interest at all in doing that. I told him I quit, and to go away. He left, and I never saw him again.

On those long walks certain scenes and words from the past came into my mind over and over. Rachel's question: *Why don't you know what Marty was wearing?* Sis's innocent little comment: *We even had to keep our coats on in class yesterday.* The judge's words when he shook my hand: *Keep her from harm, Luke.* Mom's painful words, whispered from her deathbed: *Watch over my little girl.* Sis's words the night she came back home: *I feel safe here with you, Luke ... I belong with you.* And her other words, less than a year later, her last words to me: *You're drunk.*

Saturday morning, nine days after it happened. I was lying on the couch when I heard a knock. I didn't want a visitor, but the knock persisted, so I finally got up and went to the door.

Vicky stood on the porch, holding a plate wrapped in tinfoil. "Hi, Luke."

I didn't reply, but opened the screen for her. She walked to the kitchen, and I followed. When she put the plate on the table, I said, "You've brought food over just about every day. Thank you, but that's enough. I'm all right. I can get my own food. Don't do it anymore."

She looked me in the eye and said, "You don't look all right."

"Well, I am, and anyway, it's not your problem."

"May I sit down?"

"Why?"

She pulled out a chair and sat, and pointed at the chair opposite. "Why don't you sit?"

I sat.

She leaned forward and spoke softly. "Tomorrow is Easter. They're going to have a special service, an outdoor service, where the school used to be. It's for everyone, all the churches. Will you go with me to that service, please?"

"No."

"I cannot know what you are going through. But I do know that many, many other people in this town are going through the same thing. And they will go to that service tomorrow, and they will cry with each other, and in their sorrow they will find comfort."

I grunted and looked at her. "Cry? I guess they're the lucky ones, then. I can't cry. I haven't cried since it happened. I should, but I can't. And what do you mean, comforted? How do you know that? How come you know so much?"

"Go to the service with me, Luke. Shave and put on your suit and go to the service with me."

"No, I told you. Her funeral was my last time in a church, indoor or outdoor. I don't need to hear any more about God! I know enough now! Besides, I've got other plans for tomorrow."

"To walk back and forth to her grave?"

"Well, you are a real snoop and a busybody. You just know everything, Vicky."

She looked away from me and took a deep breath. She rose and walked past me into the living room, and I got up and followed. "And don't bring any more food over," I said as she stepped onto the front porch.

She turned, and her eyes were wet. She said, "I just want you to remember something, Luke. I loved her too. I miss Marty too. You remember that." She walked to her car with her right hand at her face.

◆ ◆ ◆

On Sunday morning I got up and ate, then walked south past the Humble camp to the railroad tracks, the branch line. I walked east along the tracks for about three miles, then moved north on dirt roads I remembered from my boyhood. Ahead were derricks, marking the western edge of the oil field.

At a little rise in the road I stopped and looked around. A half-mile to the west stood a thicket of pines, and I knew that Crow Meadow lay just beyond it, to the northwest. I walked farther to a wooden bridge across a creek, then left the road and followed the creek east.

I came to the little pond. The oak tree, the rope-swing oak, still stood, its big limbs shadowing the bank. I sat under that oak, and remembered swinging the girls out over the pond, and their screams of joy.

I made my way farther down the creek, crossed it on a big pipeline, and headed north into the woods. But the woods ended before they should have. I came to the edge of a clearing. Trees had been cut and hauled away. Land had been bulldozed.

A derrick rose from the clearing, below it a producing gas well. To the left of the well was the little ridge where the fallen tree had leaned, the tree I had made into a cave with my hatchet. My tree cave, my refuge, had vanished, and in its place sat a cube of concrete, a derrick support block.

I went to the sign near the wellhead manifold.

Gulf Oil Co.

H.M. Moore #2

8-15-35

I looked on the ground for something heavy and hard. I went down the access road and found a rock six inches thick. I brought it back and heaved it again and again, rock against metal, until the sign was bent and scarred and unreadable. I walked home.

At dusk Tom Erwin knocked. I opened the door and stared at him.

"Luke, we're in grief and shock just like you, but you're family to us. Rachel and Rie want to hug you, to cry with you. Come have supper with us."

"Cry, huh? Well, they're the lucky ones. Have you cried, Tom?"

"Of course I have. My son, my boy—"

"I haven't. Not once. What kind of a man am I, Tom? I loved her, and she's gone, and I can't even cry."

"You're torn up. Come home with me, friend."

"No. I can't look at your daughter."

His eyes grew large. "She can't help it if she wasn't hurt."

"The cemetery, Tom. After the burials. I saw Rie walking back from the grave with you, and I said to myself, There's Rie, where's Marty? Yes, that's what I said, even though I'd just buried Sis. Because *never* have I seen Rie that Marty wasn't there too. I can't look at Rie, Tom. Go home."

I slammed the door and went back to the couch, and listened to Tom's slow footsteps on the porch.

◆ ◆ ◆

On Monday I came back from my second walk to the cemetery to find a note stuck in the front screen door. "Please empty your mailbox—Postman." I walked to the mailbox by the driveway and pulled out an armload of newspapers, bills, and letters. I took the pile to the kitchen table.

A dozen or so handwritten envelopes were addressed to me. Sympathy letters, I guessed, and tossed them aside. Then, another envelope, addressed to Marty. I recognized the handwriting in the center of the envelope. I looked at the upper left corner and saw, in a different handwriting,

A.E.

Oakland, Cal.

In the upper right corner of the envelope was a regular three-cent stamp, but beside it was another stamp, and this one had a picture of an airplane.

I held the envelope and stared at it, and remembered a day not long in the past. The glorious smile as she turned to look back at me, her windblown hair, her screams of joy and triumph after the landing. Then, later, her careful composition of the letter, the perfect handwriting, the hope in her eyes as she finally addressed the envelope.

I said to myself: She could be reading this, but now she can't read it, and neither will anyone else.

I went to the kitchen for a box of matches, then took the letter to the back yard. I placed the letter on a spot of bare ground and put a lit match to it. On the windless spring afternoon the light blue smoke rose straight up into the sky. I patted the black ashes into the dirt with my boot.

What caused it? Only after about twelve days did that question even enter my mind. I hadn't looked at a newspaper or listened to radio since it happened, but finally I did sit down with a paper and read an article whose headline was No Blame for School Blast, Inquiry Board Declares.

Gas had leaked from a pipe or pipes in the dead space under the main building, gas which accumulated over a period of time and then was ignited by an arc on the switch of an electric sander in the manual training shop.

The article said the original plan for heating the school called for a central steam plant, but that plan had been dropped because individual gas heaters in the rooms would cost less.

The paper also said that the use of residue gas "is considered poor policy" where so many heating units had to be adjusted because of pressure and content variations in the gas.

A court of inquiry had exonerated all school officials, and said that the explosion was the collective fault of average individuals, ignorant of or indifferent to the need for precautionary measures.

I read and re-read that article, and began to think about it on my walks to the cemetery and back. A new thought, a new regret, began to play in my head. I told myself that right after I found out about the individual heaters and the problems with the burners, I should have taken Sis out of school. Sure, she would have complained. Sure, the neighbors would have thought it strange. But she would be alive now.

Maybe other parents, hearing about what I did, would have made their own investigation. Fathers, oil men like me, would have seen the danger. A group could have gone to the school board and demanded immediate action. How different it could have been if I had only followed my instincts. What if I had spoken to Ben Halley? Maybe Ben truly had no knowledge of how dangerous the situation was. "Ignorant or indifferent," the report had said.

But I could have explained it Wednesday night. Ben was reasonable, he would have listened. "Shut off the gas at the regulator," he could have ordered the next day. So what if the kids had to wear coats in class for a week or two? The weather was already warming up.

But on Wednesday night, instead of talking to Ben about the danger, I had relaxed in a smoky, stinking honky-tonk with the drunken floozy Judy Reeves, the booze-loving alcoholic fireball

Judy. And booze-loving me had drunk right along with her, and got so drunk I couldn't even say goodnight to my little sister, and now I'd never, ever have a chance to say goodnight to her again.

❖ ❖ ❖

The next day I rested on the couch after my second walk to the graveyard when I heard footsteps on the front porch, then sobs. Rie stood at the door and wept. I stared at the floor and didn't move. Rie stayed a minute longer, then turned and stepped off the porch, her sobs louder.

I sat there for another hour, then got a few sheets of paper and a fountain pen and sat down at the kitchen table and wrote a letter.

Dear Vicky,

I am leaving, and because you have been good to me I want to tell you why.

Everything I look at in this house brings up memories of her. The chair by the fireplace where she used to sit while we listened to the radio. The kitchen sink where we washed dishes together. The radio, and her smiles and laughs at the shows. The swing, where she waited for me to get home from work.

Outside, every time I see a tree blooming, or a wild-flower, or a butterfly, or a bird, I think of what she said about those things. Even the oil derricks.

An hour ago Rie came to the door crying. I couldn't look at her. I couldn't even open the door. That's when I realized I have to leave.

I can't take these constant reminders. If I stay here, I will die. Part of me does want to die, but a part doesn't.

I need to go far away. I don't know when or if I'll be back. You are welcome to use the house, or anyone else that needs a place.

I have boxed up Marty's clothes and old toys and books. Please try to find a little girl who could use them.

You have been so good to me in the hardest and worst hours of my life, and I won't forget it. I am sorry for the way I talked to you the last time you brought food. I hope you forgive me.

You are a wonderful woman. You deserve a beautiful, happy life. The man who marries you will be a very lucky man.

Please tell the Erwins that I love them, and that I'm terribly sorry about Neil.

With friendship,

Luke

The next day at midmorning, when school was in session, I drove to Vicky's house and left the box of Marty's stuff and the letter. I went to the bank in Overton and closed my account for cash, then drove to Longview and sold my car for one hundred dollars. I took my one suitcase filled with work clothes to the T&P depot and bought a ticket. I got on a train and rode west. The green pines and the rolling hills fell away, and the land became flat and brown and dry. The train rolled on, through the day and into the night. The rhythm of the wheels put me to sleep, and when I awoke, Texas, and the life I had known, were behind me.

20

Russ

For five days Luke had talked while we worked. He had talked himself hoarse. But late Tuesday morning he came to a stopping point, a clear break. He was quiet after our noon meal.

By that time I really needed the silence. It's work listening to somebody talk. Especially when the story gets tight and tense. and you don't want to miss any words.

I've said before that I like to sing while working, and that sometimes when Luke became quiet I did sing. But I couldn't sing that afternoon. All I could do was think about his story, and the tragedy. It didn't seem a time for singing.

We had built the retaining wall and put down topsoil. Around four o'clock we began to lay squares of St. Augustine on the topsoil. Luke worked near the front walk, facing the house, and I was a few feet behind him. I heard the click of heels on the sidewalk. They stopped abruptly, and I looked up at the woman.

Soft face, dark brown hair in a bob. Blue skirt, white blouse, trim figure. I recognized her. She went to my church. But I didn't know her name.

She walked across the topsoil and stood in silence behind Luke, ignoring me. He eventually noticed her shadow and turned. He looked at her face, and his eyes grew large. He stood.

She glared at him. Even from where I knelt I could see fire in her blue eyes. Or was it ice? Yes, they can co-exist. Her stare proved it.

Luke avoided those eyes. Finally he said, "Hello, Vicky."

Silence, but I could see her chest move, and I could tell she was breathing hard. Her eyes never left his face.

Luke said, "I'm surprised you're still around. I thought you'd be … off in a city somewhere."

She stared at him and breathed faster.

He gazed to the right, then to the left, then down. I sensed an anger building. Finally he met her eyes and said, "Either talk to me or go back to your car and get outta here."

Her eyes bulged. "Oh, I'm gonna talk to you all right! I'm just trying to get control so I don't slap the—" She stopped abruptly, closed her eyes, and whispered, "Calm. Calm. Calm." Her breathing slowed, and she opened her eyes. "Not even a postcard."

Luke stared at his boots.

"We thought you were dead, of course, when the years passed, and we didn't hear anything. 'He loves us,' Rie said. 'He wouldn't do this to us if he was alive.' So we decided you'd killed yourself, or got killed. But not knowing for sure, well, that made it real hard on the Erwins, and me, and everyone else that knew you."

Luke said, "I had to—"

"Don't you dare open your mouth until I'm finished, you selfish …" She closed her eyes again and whispered, "Calm, Vicky."

She drew in a deep breath and exhaled. "Where to start? The boxes, Marty's clothes. I found a family. They were real grateful for those clothes."

Luke nodded.

"Your house. You didn't pay taxes, so the county took it over and sold it at auction. An oil man with four kids bought it. They were real happy in that house. Still are. Now the kids are all teenagers."

He nodded.

"Luke, the sun is hot. Could we sit on the porch?"

They walked up the steps and sat in the wicker chairs. Neither one paid any attention to me, so I just kept working, and listening.

Seated, she continued. "The monument. You weren't around, so they asked Tom Erwin, what name for Marty? Tom asked Rie, and Rie came to me. Rie and I became very close over the years. I told them I thought *Marty* should go on the monument, not *Martha Lee*, and she agreed."

Luke must have decided it was safe to talk, because he said, "Thank you. That's what I would have chosen."

"Have you seen the monument?"

"No."

"Just where *have* you been, Luke?" Her voice had not lost the sharp edge.

"Northwest. Washington."

"About as far from us as you could get, huh?"

He stared into the street.

She asked, "Why did you come back?"

"To visit her grave."

"Well, you've obviously done that, so why are you still here? Why are you working with Russ?"

"Met him at the cemetery. He needed some help with the railroad ties. We're almost through with this job, so I'll be going back north. Vicky?"

"Yes?"

"Tell me about Rie. Where is she?"

"You weren't very interested in Rie when it happened. Why are you interested now?"

Silence. Vicky finally said, "She and Seth got married right before the war started. Seth Lacefield is a farm boy who went to Rie's church. Came through the explosion unhurt, just like her. He went to war, fought in the Pacific, Guadalcanal, Tarawa. Rie had his baby, a little girl, while he was gone. He was a hero, brought home a lot of combat medals. He stayed in the Marines. He and Rie live in San Diego. They have a little boy now too."

Her voice had softened, anger melted to sadness.

Luke said, "Well, I guess you have children of your own."

"I'm not married."

His eyebrows went up. "Well, I find that hard to believe. Pretty woman, smart woman. That is very surprising."

"I've had offers."

"You live here in Henderson?"

"New London. I still teach there."

"A woman like you, staying in a little town like that. Doesn't make sense to me."

"I like to teach. It's a good school. What *you* did doesn't make sense."

After a pause Luke asked, "How did you know I was here?"

"My cousin told me. He lives here in Henderson. Drove by yesterday and recognized you. You remember my cousin's name, Luke?"

A pause, then "Kelly."

"You remember."

"Yes, I remember that afternoon. I remember the laughter. But I remember another afternoon too, and that other afternoon wiped out everything, the laughter, the past, everything. And that's why I had to leave. I know you hate me for it, but I just had to do it."

Vicky stood. "Rie told me if I ever heard anything about you to let her know right away, so I need to go down to the telegraph office."

Luke stood, and they walked down the steps together to the sidewalk. She reached in her purse for car keys and said, "Well, good luck."

"It was nice to see you again."

She stared at the keys. "Would you like to go to church with me on Sunday?"

Luke seemed surprised, even angry. "I don't go to church. Her funeral was my last time in a church. Besides, I'll probably be gone by Sunday."

She fingered the keys. "If you change your mind, I sit on the third pew from the front, on the left. Same place every Sunday. Creature of habit. Old maid schoolmarm and creature of habit."

She walked toward her car, then turned.

"Luke?"

"What?"

"Get rid of the beard."

She drove away, her eyes fixed on the road ahead.

Was there more to Luke's story? I wasn't sure until later that day. We finished laying the sod about six and drove home. I found a note on my door. Lady in Tyler wanted me to put a large rock garden in her yard. I asked Luke if he could help me a couple of more days. He said he would, so I knew the story wasn't over.

We drove to Tyler the next morning, and the lady explained what she wanted. I figured it for a two-day job. I was glad Luke had stayed, because we ended up hauling some pretty heavy rocks.

21

Luke

Ever been out west, Russ, way out west? Out past West Texas and New Mexico and Arizona? No? That's where I went that spring. I rode the rails all the way to the Pacific Ocean. Got on a train in Longview and stepped off in Los Angeles, California. I crossed a lot of deserts, but at the end of the deserts I found a big oasis.

Los Angeles. You'd have to see it to believe it. Of course I'd never been in a town bigger than Tyler, so I guess the size of the place shocked me more than it would some people. But it wasn't just the size. Would you believe that spring lasts all through the summer? It's never hot there, never humid. Never rains in the summer either, but you wouldn't know it by looking at all the orchards and flowers and palm trees.

I found a rooming house. I went to some garages to try to find work. The men looked at me like I was nuts. Some of 'em cursed me under their breath. "Go back to Texas. They got cars there, don't they?" one fellow told me.

With all the oil jobs in East Texas I had forgotten about the Depression. But it hadn't ended. Things were bad in California.

I quit trying to find work. I spent the days riding streetcars.

Los Angeles had red streetcars that went all over, far out from the center of the city. I'd ride the streetcars to the distant towns, then back, over and over.

Sometimes in the evening I'd ride to a place called Santa Monica, on the ocean. You could go out on a pier and watch the sun set. I'd stand there and watch that orange ball sink into the blue waters. I got to thinking: Marty would have a lot to say about this sunset, this ocean, this town, this weather, these people. She might even want to stay here. Why would she want to leave the palm trees and beaches and movie studios and mountains and ocean breezes?

No, Sis would love it here, I decided. She would become a California girl. And when Rie and Annie came out on the train to visit, Marty would show them the sights. I'd drive, of course. Me in the front seat and the three girls in the back, and I'd listen to their chatter and their laughter. I'd drive them to the beaches, to the parks, to the hills, to Hollywood, to San Juan Capistrano, maybe even all the way down to San Diego to ride the roller coaster.

With Sis, I could stay. I could find work if I had to. But I didn't have to. My money was running out, but no one depended on me.

Time to move on, I decided. Los Angeles was not far enough away from what I needed to leave. Too many people, too many women, too many young girls with tanned and smiling faces, too many flowers, too many orchards, too much sunshine. I needed a very different environment. I wasn't sure what it was. I had to keep looking.

I wandered the streets and spoke to men who looked like they survived on little or no money. I learned about places where men on the move gathered. I traded my suitcase for a canvas bag and packed it with a coat, a change of clothes, those pictures of Sis, and a few other items. I left the rooming house one early fall morning and walked a few miles to the Southern Pacific rail yard. I found the hobo camp and learned what I needed to know. Late that afternoon I ran toward an open boxcar as a northbound freight train pulled out of the yard. A dozen or so other men did the same thing.

The pleasant city of Los Angeles faded away, and a desert took its place. I knew then the environment I was seeking—a cold, dark desert. As the train rumbled north, I felt pangs of hunger, and Rachel's question sounded over and over in my mind, like the clack of steel wheels on rail: *Why don't you know what Marty was wearing?* And I felt like I needed, deserved, the pain those words brought me.

I became a tramp that winter. Hobo, bum, whatever. There were a lot of us on the road looking for work, but work's pretty scarce in the farm country in the winter. If we couldn't find work, we at least tried to find food and shelter.

The government had set up relief camps here and there. I couldn't stand those places, because of the families that stayed in them. Families, from Oklahoma, Texas, Arkansas, Missouri. People who had left their failing farms to come west. People that talked the same way I did. You might think I'd have liked being with them, but I didn't. Because they had something I didn't have—spirit. Some of the locals called them "Okies," but they weren't defeated. They looked forward to the spring. They talked about the miles and miles of cotton fields. They were strong people. But they had each other, that's why. The men had the women. The kids had the parents. The brothers and sisters had each other. I didn't have anybody, and I resented those strong and hope-filled families. Only desperate hunger forced me to the relief camps.

I moved north on the freight trains through California's big central valley. A week in Bakersfield, a few days in Visalia, then Fresno for a week, then Stockton. I found work here and there, digging drainage ditches, that sort of thing. My size and strength got me jobs other men couldn't handle.

But I kept moving north. The days shortened, and the nights became long and cold. Sacramento, Marysville, Chico, Redding, a few days at most in any one place. I learned the ways of the tramps, but made no friends and never spoke of my past.

I learned how to beg for food. I'd shave and comb my hair and walk into town. I'd look for houses with families. I'd knock on the door, and when it opened I'd take off my hat and ask if I could work for a meal. About one in three times I'd come away with something, a sandwich, an apple, a boiled egg or two, and now and then small change.

A few times lonely ladies invited me in for a meal. They tried to talk to me. I ate their food, thanked them, and left.

I got up to Dunsmuir, to a rail yard. Two routes to Eugene, said the trackside tramps. Don't go the west route. Mostly slow lumber trains. Take the east route to Klamath Falls. Flip a manifest and get north in a hurry. Dress warm, and take food and water.

I moved through Oregon in early '38. Klamath Falls, over the Cascades to Eugene, then Salem, and finally Portland. I hung around Portland for a while, and that's where I heard about the dam. The more I thought about it, the more I wanted to go to that dam. But it wasn't an easy place to get to.

I crossed into Washington, to the town of Vancouver. I spent two days lying low in the Spokane, Portland and Seattle Railroad yard. I learned which tracks held eastbound trains, and got to know the rituals of the railroad bulls.

The second night I found the boxcar I wanted, and when the

sun rose the next day, that boxcar and I were moving east. South of the tracks was the river I'd crossed to get to Vancouver. It was a mighty big river, deep blue and wide, but I didn't even know its name. Above the river were mountains, dark green and tall.

In a few hours the mountains disappeared. The land became brown and flat, without features except for the river. In late afternoon the train slowed, and I saw a town up ahead. I tossed my bag to the ground, eased myself feet-first out the boxcar door, and hit the ground running.

Kennewick, said the sign on a nearby road. I found the hobo camp and the men shared their stew. I told them where I wanted to go, and they told me to hitchhike. I asked the name of the river. A couple of 'em laughed and asked where I was from. It's the Columbia, they told me.

I hitchhiked north. A day later, at a little town called Wilbur, I got final directions. The sun had set, but the moon rose full, so I kept walking. Only twenty-five miles, they had told me at the store.

The moon, bright and sharp in that cold desert air, moved west. I moved north. I'd stop and rest now and then, but I kept moving, totally alone on the gravel road.

The eastern sky turned a pale blue, and soon the sun's arc topped the horizon. I cast a long shadow westward. My legs ached. I was thirsty and hungry.

Then I crossed a low hill and saw it. My pulse quickened. One more hill for a clearer view. I topped the last hill.

In the middle of that treeless, windswept desert flowed the big river whose name I now knew. But in its channel was a low, huge concrete mass. Cranes towered above the concrete and cables stretched over the water. Across the river, smoke rose from the chimneys of a town.

I knew that the place was called Grand Coulee, and that men

were building a dam, the biggest dam ever. In the cold desert men worked with a goal, to stop the river's flow. I decided to join those men, and help them build the dam. My life could go on. Sis didn't need me any more, but now I had a purpose—help men pour concrete to hold back a mighty river.

22

Russ

*L*uke usually said little in the evenings, but always had a comment on the meal. On Wednesday night, after our first day of working the rock garden, I fixed sliced ham, fried okra, mashed potatoes and gravy, onions, pear slices. It was a tasty supper, and I expected a word or two from Luke.

But on this night he ate in silence until we were almost finished. Then he said, "Yesterday morning when I talked about Marty's funeral, I looked over at you, and your hands were shaking. Why?"

I took a drink of tea to give me a chance to think, then said, "Arms must have been tired from the shoveling."

He grunted. "Your arms don't get tired. Something bothered you when I talked about the funeral."

I forced myself to keep eating.

"It happened on Thursday. The funerals were Saturday. Were you there on Saturday, Russ?"

My mind raced. I sensed he would not accept silence. He didn't.

"Did you know one of the kids that died? Grandchild? Friend of grandchild?"

I shook my head.

"But you were there in New London on that day?"

I swallowed and nodded.

"So whose funeral did you go to?"

I forced down a last bite of okra.

He persisted. "Where was this hospital you worked at, and what did you do there?"

I looked up. "Can't a man have a secret?"

"I won't tell anyone your secret. I'm going north when we finish the job. Your secret's safe. So, whose funeral did you go to?"

"I don't know."

"What do you mean, you don't know?"

"Just what I said."

His voice rose. "Where was the hospital, and what did you do there?"

Another crossroads. I could order Luke out of the house. Would serve him right for his rude questioning. Drive him to Longview and drop him off at the rail yard. Finish the rock garden on my own. But then I'd never hear the rest of *his* story. And I needed to hear that story.

Maybe he was right. He'd be leaving soon, and I didn't care if anyone in Seattle knew the secret.

"All right, Luke. The hospital was in Rusk. What did I do? Well, they gave the patients little jobs. I folded laundry, swept, mopped."

He stared at me, expressionless.

I said, "You've been away for a while, but you remember about Rusk, don't you?"

His brow furrowed. "Yeah, I remember. Mental hospital."

I nodded. "Rusk State Hospital. But you need to hear the whole story. Leave the dishes, let's go out on the back porch, there's a little breeze tonight."

I didn't look forward to talking on a full stomach. I'd rather read or listen to the radio. But I had chosen the path, and there was no going back.

We took our seats. "Luke, I had a nickname for a long time. Want to guess what it was?"

"No."

"My nickname was Gabby. Gabby Smith, that's what they called me. Not a joke, either. Very descriptive."

"Wouldn't have guessed it."

"You asked me why I never sang in a church choir. The reason was, the choir was always behind me."

"So?"

"I stood in the pulpit. Forty years a pastor. Reverend Gabby Smith. I could talk the day long."

23

Russ

For me it all started in Paris, Texas. I was born and raised there. My daddy had a drayage business. He was always buying and trading mules and horses and fixing wagons.

I was around fourteen years old when I realized I had a talent, if you want to call it that, for speaking. I had a deep, clear voice that projected well. I liked it when people turned their eyes and ears to me. The more they listened, the more I wanted to say. And the bigger the crowd of listeners, the better.

I never thought about being anything but a preacher. Some folks back then told me I should go into law. Pays well, they told me. Well, a lot of men who like to hear themselves talk do go into that arena, but it wasn't for me. I figured out that a lawyer gets to talk to a crowd only when a court lets him, whereas a preacher has more or less regular opportunities to make himself heard.

At age eighteen I was preaching in North Texas churches, and by age twenty I had my own church. About that time a young lady came into my life. Mabel Foster was a tall, brown-haired farm girl, an only child. When I first started to court her, I made the mistake of trying to impress her by talking. I learned real quick that she didn't care for that. One day I was driving her in the buggy from church back to the farmhouse, gabbing away, when all of a sudden she reached over and put her index finger against my lips. And when I became quiet, she scooted over a little closer to me and just briefly put her head on my shoulder. Well, I thought that was very bold for a seventeen-year-old girl. But that pretty head on my shoulder felt good. And I learned that Mabel didn't need to hear me talk to enjoy my company. We got married a few months later.

By age twenty-five I had a wife, a baby, and a nickname: Gabby Smith. People liked me. People like a good talker, Luke.

I had found satisfaction. I looked around me and saw a lot of men not sure of what they wanted to do, changing jobs, trying this, trying that. I went about my business with joy. Comforting, advising, uplifting.

Gabby was a talking machine. I could talk all the daylight hours. I could talk without even thinking!

We ended up down in Nacogdoches County. I had several churches around there and pastored the last one, in Nacogdoches, for thirteen years. I turned sixty ten years ago. I had three grown children, six grandchildren, and a loving wife. No man could have wanted more. Then it all changed, in one day.

I'll never forget that Thursday night when we got the news about the school at New London. Hundreds dead, children and teachers. We went to bed horrified and sickened.

At noon the next day I got a phone call. They're gonna have individual funerals, a man told me. They need preachers to work in shifts, some in the churches, some at graveside. Can you preach four funerals, one hour's worth? he asked me. I said yes, and he said to be there at nine-thirty in the morning.

I left home the next day prepared to do the job. I had averaged about two funerals a month over my forty years. A thousand or so funerals, and four more coming up.

I had just passed through Henderson when a headache came on all of a sudden. Sharp, stabbing pain. I pulled off the road and lay down in the front seat. Must have lain there twenty or thirty minutes.

Finally the pain started to ease. Sweat soaked my shirt. But I had a job to do. I drove on to New London to the church.

I parked and walked toward the door to the vestibule, ready to introduce myself. A man approached me, and when I shook his and tried to say my name, the words came out a mumble. I felt the headache return.

The man said something to me and handed me a sheet of paper. I got the idea it was time for the service to begin. Apparently my earlier stop due to the headache had caused me to arrive at the church just prior to the service.

I assumed the sheet of paper had the name of the child whose funeral I was to preach, and the names of the child's parents. I pulled out my own notes, prepared the night before.

I stepped to the pulpit as the pianist finished a familiar hymn. I looked down at my notes and felt a sting of fear. For on those pages were not words, but strange black marks.

The other paper, the one that man handed me, had a similar collection of black marks. Somehow my ability to read had vanished.

A bad situation, but in that sanctuary were people who had suffered a far greater loss, so I didn't spend any time feeling sorry for myself. I knew I could talk my way through it. Believe it or not, I had once preached the funeral of a man whose name escaped me when I got to the pulpit having no notes. I preached anyway, and the family later told me they were deeply moved by the beautiful tribute. So I knew it was not absolutely necessary to say the name of the deceased. Gabby could pull it off.

As I pondered how to begin, a fresh terror swept over me. For not only could I not read words, I could not *recall* any words! Gabby, who could talk without thinking, could not come up with a single word!

I pulled out a handkerchief and wiped my brow. A man stepped up and handed me a cup of water. I prayed. Prayer without words, but God would understand. I prayed for a word, any word, to come into my mind.

I don't know how long I stood up there. Probably no more than a couple of minutes. I couldn't look at the family sitting in front of me. Finally I stepped down, made my way out of the church to my car, and drove home, my heart pounding through every mile.

Mabel knew something was wrong when she first saw me. She spoke to me, but I didn't understand her. I just shook my head.

She drove me to the hospital. I couldn't understand the doctors and nurses. They took me to a room—I think it was in the psychiatric ward. A doctor came and showed me some words in big block letters. Next to the words were pictures. I inferred that he wanted me to match the words to the pictures. The doctor seemed to get impatient and stood up like he was gonna to leave, but I grabbed his arm and moaned. I didn't want him to leave until he understood my problem. His face tightened, and he said something to a nurse. A minute later, two orderlies came in, jerked me up, and put me in a straightjacket. They took it off later, after putting me in a locked room for the night.

Mabel came the next day and spoke to me very tenderly. I couldn't understand her, but it didn't matter. Her tone, her gentleness, her eyes conveyed her love much better than any words could have. She wept before leaving, and I sensed that we would be apart for some time.

They committed me to Rusk State Hospital. I knew it was

wrong, but I had no way of protesting. All I could hope was that my voice would come back, soon.

After a few weeks in that hospital, I began to feel that my life was over. The word "alone" takes on a whole new meaning when you can't communicate. A dark despair fell over me like a thick, suffocating blanket. I had been abandoned by the world and by God, apparently.

Everything was white in that place. The walls, the floors, the ceilings, the beds, the uniforms, all white. But to me it couldn't have been blacker.

They put me on a ward and taught me how to do little jobs. I swept, mopped, folded laundry. I ate three meals a day with fellow patients in a lunch room. Some of the patients talked to each other during the day. They ignored me, since I never spoke.

I wondered why some of those patients were in the hospital. They seemed normal to me. Maybe it's best that I couldn't understand what they said.

Every few days a nurse sat down with me and showed me pictures and words, to see if I could tell her what I saw. I couldn't.

The hours fell away, the days, the weeks. I dreaded waking up. Time moved on while sleep held me, but slowed to a pitiful crawl during the endless daylight. Without a reason to live, I began to long for death. And I might have died, if that gardener hadn't whistled one afternoon.

When the weather permitted, we were allowed outdoors for a while each day. I usually went to one of the picnic tables and sat. From an oak tree in the courtyard I sometimes heard songs of birds. One afternoon I heard a different sound, a man whistling. A gardener, kneeling over a bed of flowers beside the building, whistled while he worked. And I recognized the tune.

At that moment three blessed words came into my head, words that went with the tune. The words "Rescue the perishing."

My heart leaped for joy. I tried to speak the words. I couldn't, but it didn't bother me. One thing at a time. Three words lingered in my head. God had not abandoned me.

I replayed the tune mentally, day and night. What words came next? A week later they came to me: "Care for the dying." Four more jewels.

A week later: "Snatch them in pity from sin and the grave."

A few days after that: "Weep o'er the erring one, Lift up the fallen, Tell them of Jesus the mighty to save."

A whole stanza. Words treasured beyond words. Then one night a name came to me. Fanny Crosby. A blind poet's words relearned by a man who couldn't speak.

Over and over the tune played in my head, and pretty soon I recalled another stanza.

> Down in the human heart, crushed by the tempter,
> Feelings lie buried that grace can restore;
> Touched by a loving heart, wakened by kindness,
> Chords that were broken will vibrate once more.

I still couldn't read or write either, so how could I let the nurses, the doctors, know what had happened? I decided not to even try, but to relax and try to recall some other tunes. It worked. The songs came back to me, first the tunes, then the words: "My hope is built on nothing less," "leaning on the everlasting arms," "Savior, more than life to me." One after another they came back.

Then one day something very strange happened. I still don't understand it. I had words in my head, from the songs, but I couldn't get them out. But instead of trying to *say* those words, I decided to try to *sing* the songs themselves. And it worked! When I sang, the words did come out, very mumbled and jumbled at first, hard for anyone to understand, but they came out!

I started to sing everywhere, in the dining room, in the wash room, in the halls, in the courtyard. Now in any normal setting, people would have thought I was nuts, singing words that nobody could understand. But this was a mental hospital, so nobody paid any attention to me at all. Just old Russ making strange noises, they must have said.

But with practice the words became clearer, and eventually the staff began to take notice. They must have thought it was very odd that I could sing but not talk. But they started working with me. It was a beginning, but a long journey lay ahead. They started me off like a first-grader. I learned the shapes of letters. In a few weeks I was able to read, out loud, with agonizing slowness, simple stories from a first-grade reader. I kept singing too. Seems like I needed the singing to keep my spirits up.

I moved on to second grade. It took me about a month to pass through each grade. I will tell you this—learning to talk from scratch is harder than you could ever imagine, unless you had to do it. But after a year I could hold an adult conversation, and I could read.

Thirteen months after my admission, I sat down with a doctor, and he handed me a sheet of paper with a single word on it. I didn't recognize the word and for a horrible second thought I'd regressed. The word was "aphasia." The doctor said it was the word for my earlier condition. He said my headache the morning of the funeral had been caused by a stroke, and the stroke had cut off blood from a part of the brain that deals with words, and it had taken a year to "retrain" my brain. He sort of apologized for the fact that I had been diagnosed as mentally ill, and he said that my experience, which would be shared with other doctors, would help advance medical knowledge. I guess that should have made me feel better, but it didn't.

They discharged me. But the man who walked out of Rusk State Hospital was not the man who had walked in. Gabby had died. Now I had to think before I spoke, and my words came out slowly. But the odd thing is, it didn't bother me. I didn't want to be Gabby again.

I had a lot of time to think during those thirteen months. Many idle hours. I got to thinking about the man I'd been. Gabby had a gift, all right, but he wasted it. Words are precious. You realize that when you have to learn to talk all over again. Gabby's words went from memory straight to mouth. He tossed out words like confetti.

The stroke had taken Gabby away. Who was left? I didn't know.

My sons drove me to my daughter's house in Dallas. I had been aware, over the past several months, that Mabel's health had declined, but I wasn't prepared for what greeted me. She lay in a bed, terribly thin, wasted by disease. But she recognized me, and when she heard me say words, I could see a light in those tired eyes.

We talked, over the next few days. I sat by the bed and held her hand, and we talked about the old days and our good long life together. Finally she left this world, right in front of my eyes. And I kept thinking of the pretty young girl who put her finger on my lips.

After we buried her, I went back to Nacogdoches. We had lived there for many years and had many friends, or so I thought. On a Sunday morning I went to the church where I used to preach. People shook my hand, but the looks I got gave me chills. People whispered. I heard the word "Rusk" mumbled. Children pointed at me and giggled.

I had gone there thinking that someone would invite me to Sunday dinner. But after the service no one approached me.

The realization hit me that not only had Gabby died, but so had the life he had led. To the people who had known Gabby, I was the pastor who had lost his mind. The preacher who had gone nuts, and had to be taken to Rusk State Hospital. *Stay away from him, children. He doesn't talk the same anymore. Why did they let him out?* I could read the unspoken words in their faces. Sometimes faces are easier to read than letters on a page.

That afternoon I drove back to the town where I first couldn't talk. I saw a new school building where the old one once stood. I drove out to Pleasant Hill Cemetery and wandered among the graves, looking at the names and dates. So many new headstones with the same date—March 18, 1937. The question suddenly hit me: Whose funeral had I failed to preach? What child's name was on that piece of paper that I couldn't read?

I stood in that cemetery while the sun went down and wondered why God took away my voice on the morning I was to give comfort to grieving families. And why did he let Gabby go on for so long? For forty years I'd had a certainty about life, God, my purposes, everything. Now the only certainty was uncertainty.

The next day I found this little house, vacated by a recent death. I bought it. My wife and I had saved some money over the years.

When my children heard about it, they almost had me committed again. My daughter begged me to come live with her. They were angry, but I had chosen my path. I moved in. I put in the vegetable garden out back, and the rose gardens on the sides. I found I liked working outdoors.

When my neighbors asked, I told them I was from Paris, Texas, and was a retired gardener and landscaper. I had little else to say to them. They left me alone.

For a year or so I rarely ventured out, except to visit my children twice a year. But something began to gnaw at me. The songs that had saved me in the hospital—the tunes and words that had come back to me and led to my recovery—I felt a need to actually *hear* them again. And the only place where that could happen was church.

One Sunday I put on my suit and went to the church where I had failed to preach that funeral. Why that particular church? I will never know. Something drew me there. I kind of sneaked in after the service had started. I sat on the back pew. I prayed no one would recognize me, and no one appeared to. I scooted out during the final hymn. During the next week I found myself singing the songs I had sung on Sunday morning.

I joined that church. Now I sit on the back row, and sing when everybody else sings. And I listen to the preacher, and often I shake my head and say to myself: Did Gabby really say things like *that*? I don't socialize with the other folks. I leave right after the service.

One day I drove through one of the oil camps north of here. I saw the rows of stark little white houses where the oil workers and their families live. Bare yards. Colorless, like oil field camps everywhere. I got to thinking how easy it would be to bring a little beauty to those camps.

One spring day while the men were at work and the children in school, I drove to a camp and knocked on doors and talked to the ladies. I offered to put in shrubs and flowers to brighten their yards. When they said they couldn't afford it, I said I wouldn't charge for the labor. Some of them couldn't find a reason to say no.

The greenery and flowers around those homes drew attention. The women were happy, and that made the men happy, and the men gave me a few dollars for my time. Other people contacted me. Soon the camps were not bland and stark anymore but had some color and variety.

I developed a reputation: Russ, the gardener who sings while he works. Over the years the reputation spread. I got jobs in all the towns around here—New London, Henderson, Arp, Troup, Kilgore, even Tyler. I got into landscaping as well as gardening. And two years ago when the caretaker at Pleasant Hill died, the cemetery committee offered me that job, and I took it. My spring and summer days fill up.

As far as I'm aware, not a single person around here knows of my year in a mental hospital. I remember the looks on those faces in Nacogdoches. And those people had known me and liked me for years. It would be the same here, if someone were to find out. There's something very frightening to people about a mental patient, especially a pastor. God's not supposed to treat a pastor that way, is He? So the people question God and the pastor both.

Luke, keep my secret.

24

I slept well after telling the story, and woke up rested and hungry. Not having to hide something can really brighten your attitude.

I wolfed down the eggs, bacon, and toast, but Luke didn't seem to have an appetite. He didn't say a word all through breakfast. Just sipped his coffee and nibbled at a toast. Something simmered in his mind. The look on his face reminded me of the angry man at the cemetery.

We drove on to Tyler. The rocks were in place, and today we'd put in the topsoil and plant the rose bushes. We drove to the nursery and got a load of dirt, then headed back to the garden. Luke stood in the bed of the truck and shoveled the dirt out, and I smoothed it with a rake.

I expected Luke would start on his story. I was curious about what he did at that dam. But he didn't say a word, just shoveled the topsoil.

Eventually the silence pulled a song out of me; I think it was "Saved by Grace." An hour passed, and still no words from Luke. We drove to the nursery for another load of dirt.

More silence as we worked with shovel and rake. Around ten o'clock I felt the need to sing again.

> There's a wideness in God's mercy,
> Like the wideness of the sea;
> There's a kindness in his justice,
> Which is more than liberty.
> There is no place where earth's sorrows
> Are more felt than up in heaven;
> There is no place—

All of a sudden a shovel flew past my face, clanged against a rock, and bounced back toward me. Luke leaped from the truck bed, his fists clinched and his eyes bulging.

"I've had it. You and your stupid hymns. There's one hymn you don't sing, though. My hymn! I used to know the words. Something like 'All things bright and beautiful, the Lord God made them all.' I sang that when I was a little boy. My baby sister was bright and beautiful. The most beautiful thing ever. So why did He let her die? She was thirteen years old! You tell me, Pastor!"

Cold hatred filled his eyes. My heart raced with fear that he would hit me. But I knew better than to say anything.

He jabbed a finger at my face. "What was Gabby gonna say up there in that pulpit, Russ? Yeah, Gabby had notes! What were you gonna say to that family? How were you gonna comfort them? Tell me!"

I met his eyes. "Gabby's been gone a long time. I don't know what he was going to say. It's like he was another person. I don't remember his words."

He cursed me again. "Then what would *you* say? Forget Gabby. You go to church. You sing the hymns. What would you have said to that family?"

I shook my head. "I don't know. I'm not a pastor anymore. I don't belong in a pulpit. I'm a gardener and landscaper."

He glared at me, then spat at my feet. He picked up the shovel. "If I hear another hymn today I'm gonna crack this shovel across your face." He jumped back into the bed of the truck and started shoveling the dirt out.

I picked up the rake and began to smooth the dirt. We worked in silence, and when I glanced at him I could still see rage on his face.

After we put in the rose bushes, the lady brought her friend to see our work. The friend liked it and asked me if we could do the same thing in her yard.

I almost said no right off the bat. I didn't want Luke around anymore. I feared him. I knew he had come close to hitting me.

But I didn't have a good excuse for turning the woman down, and I don't like making up lies. So I told her yes.

After she left, Luke approached me. I tensed up, expecting another outburst, but he said, "Got us another job, huh? Yeah, I'll stay and help. You're not gonna get rid of me that easy. And you *will* answer my question, Pastor, whether you want to or not. So you better think about how you plan to do that."

Supper that night was downright unpleasant. I like silence during a meal, but not when anger floats over the table. I had no appetite, and went to bed early.

Sometimes a night's sleep can smooth away the edges of a rage, but at breakfast I saw that Luke's anger had not lessened. His movements were like those of a snake coiling to strike. I almost wanted him to erupt in curses. I could handle that, but not the awful tension of waiting for a violent explosion.

We hauled and stacked rocks during the morning, saying only

enough to get the job done. But during a rest break the silence got to me again, and without thinking I started to sing.

> *Come, ye sinners, poor and needy,*
> *Weak and wounded, sick and sore;*
> *Jesus ready stands—*

I caught myself and jerked my head toward Luke. He glared at me. I breathed faster and wiped my brow. I needed to stay alert. These were dangerous moments.

I gave myself a command—no singing. I obeyed that command for another half-hour. But then my mind seemed to forget. Something inside me said, Fill the silence with a song. I sang.

> *What I am, Thine eye can see,*
> *Yet I come, O Lord, to Thee,*
> *Though my sins are crimson red,*
> *Yet for me Thy—*

I gulped and turned. Luke, fifteen feet away, held a big rock. He started toward me, then tossed the rock to the ground.

"There's only one way I'm gonna get you to stop singing. You only sing when it's quiet, so I guess I'll have to talk. I'll tell you about a man you remind me of. He was a little bit like me, but a lot more like you. He irritated me. He found my private ledge above the river, and he tried to tell me about God."

25

Luke

I crossed over that final hill and looked down on the dam in the spring of 1938. My timing couldn't have been better. The dam's foundation had been finished a few months earlier, but the government decided to change contractors, so a lot of the fellows who'd worked on the foundation were gone. The new contractor needed men. When I explained my background to the folks at the hiring office, they were pleased. They were short of mechanics, they said. Lots of trucks and cranes and bulldozers to keep running. Skilled labor, one-twenty-five an hour.

I didn't have the twenty-five bucks for union dues, but they said they'd loan it to me and take it out of my paycheck a little at a time. Report to the motor pool, they told me. Need a place to bed down? Town of Grand Coulee, that's where the single men stay. Lots of dormitories and bunkhouses. Plenty of places to have a good time after work too.

I found a dollar-a-night bunkhouse and joined the motor pool. The other mechanics called me "Tex." There weren't many people from the South at the dam.

At night I'd wander around that ramshackle town, past the pool halls and dance halls and taverns and whorehouses. I'd hear laughter and curses and out-of-tune pianos. I'd see drunken men fighting in the streets. I never stopped to watch.

Sometimes I'd walk out into the desert. In summer the wind blew dust all the time, day and night.

Grand Coulee—rough, dirty, and desolate. Men without women, far from cities and comfort. Just the environment I had been looking for.

I got along okay with most of my coworkers, but this one mechanic named Preston took a dislike to me. I guess he mistook my silence for arrogance. Preston was a little shorter than me, and had a barrel chest and thick, hairy arms.

One summer afternoon we were waiting for the bus to take us back to town when Preston walked up with two other men. "Hey, Tex. Come on down to the Swanee Rooms with us tonight. They got some new girls down there. We'll have a few drinks on the first floor, then go up to the second floor. How about it?"

Well, if I'd wanted to go to that kind of place I'd have gone alone, not with Preston. I shook my head. "No, thanks."

Preston turned to the men with him. "Either he don't like our company, or he's a sissy."

He turned back toward me, and my left fist cracked into his chin. He stumbled backwards. I said, "Don't call me names. Tex is okay, but no other names."

Blood came from his lower lip, and rage filled his face. "Hick, I'm gonna knock you back to Texas." The other men spread out to give us room.

He charged, and we both went to the ground, but I was up first. You know, Russ, it's funny. I hadn't fought since I was a boy, but there's some things you don't forget. I knew I could take him. He came at me again, and those arms were like flying sledgehammers, but he didn't know how to protect himself from a left hand, and sure enough I got in a hard shot to his cheek, and he went down.

I guess the word spread about that fight, because nobody ever bothered me again. The men respected me and left me alone.

◆ ◆ ◆

Around August of that year I started thinking about women. How long had it been since I'd touched a woman? Who did I touch last? Judy? No. Vicky? No, Rachel, at the cemetery. She fell into my arms. Rachel, seventeen months earlier.

I went to this place called the Silver Dollar. I sat at the bar, sipped a drink, and listened to piano music from the dancing area. I finished the drink and ordered a second.

I gazed past the end of the bar to the dance hall. Two girls sat at a table, and a tall brunette came from across the room to join them. I kept my eye on the brunette.

The piano player started a slow ballad. I finished the second drink, slid off the barstool, and walked to the table where the girls sat. I caught the brunette's eye and smiled. "Would you like to dance?"

She stood and held her right hand palm upward. I stared at her hand, then at her gray eyes. "Well?"

"Well, where's your dime?" Her smile seemed as forced as my own.

"Sign above the door says free dancing."

The girls laughed, and the brunette said, "Sure it's free. No cover charge to get in here. Bring your own girl, and you can dance all night. But you want to dance with us, it's ten cents a dance. Our time's worth that much, don't you think?"

I pulled two nickels from my pocket. "That song's half over. I get another full song after this." She nodded, and I put the nickels in her hand and guided her onto the dance floor.

Ten dances later I knew that her name was Alice, that she had worked as a taxi dancer for four months, and that she was hoping to save enough money to go back to Spokane and enroll in secretarial school.

I liked her voice, her smile, her shape, her scent. I offered to buy her a drink, and she told me that the owner wouldn't let them drink with customers, but that tomorrow when she got off work at ten, she'd take me up on the drink. I agreed to meet her.

But in my bunk that night I changed my mind. Alice was a decent girl who had no business in a hole like Grand Coulee. She needed to be back in Spokane, with decent people. Why encourage her to stay by dating her? I might like her, and turn on the charm, and it might work, and she might start to like me. And that wouldn't be good for her or for me.

No, Alice needed to leave. I'd never go back to the Silver Dollar. I'd down my whiskeys in another bar. Plenty of places to drink in Grand Coulee.

Several years would go by before I touched another woman.

My past was another time, another world. Only at night did that world come back to me. I tried to push the past away, but learned that dreams are beyond control. I dreamed of pine forests and oil derricks and red dirt roads. I dreamed of a white house, and a rope swing over a pond, and a cave made from a tree. I dreamed of a little girl growing up, a little girl who loved me.

The years passed, and the dam rose, higher and higher above the river. Building a dam in the middle of a desert was not easy. A lot of the men quit after six months or a year and went back to the cities and farms and small towns. Back to women, families, and normalcy. Back to where the wind didn't blow dust all day long.

I stayed. I became the old-timer in the motor pool. The other mechanics came to me with the tough problems.

I grew accustomed to the loneliness, the cold and long winter nights and the hot, dry, and dusty summer days. I came to depend on the monotonous routines of daily existence.

The dam fascinated me. On Sunday, my day off, I'd walk down and look at the dam and the river. I walked the rim of the canyon trying to find good vantage points. One day, about a mile downriver from the dam, I found a flat ledge on the canyon wall, about thirty feet long, not visible from the road above. I could sit on that ledge and lean against the canyon wall and look at the dam. At one end of the ledge, an overhang above three large rocks formed a little enclosure, and I found that I could stretch out in the enclosure and close my eyes and sometimes fall asleep.

One day I woke from a nap and saw a man sitting at the other end of the ledge, looking down at the river. I sat up, but didn't say anything. In a few minutes he got up to leave, noticed me, and walked over.

Looked to be in his early forties. Glasses and brown thinning hair. Government engineer, I guessed.

He smiled. "You sure found a good spot."

"Yeah. Took me two months to find it. So don't tell anybody. Wouldn't want a crowd here."

He laughed. "Funny you say that. I've been looking for a good spot too. I can stare at that thing for hours." He nodded toward the dam. Then he put out his hand. "I'm Bob Coleman."

"Luke Robertson." We shook.

"Nice to meet you. Well, I better get home. Say, you wouldn't mind if I come here on Sunday sometimes, would you?"

"I don't own it."

"I won't tell anyone. Are you from Oklahoma, Luke?"

"Texas."

"Well, that's pretty close. Maybe see you next week."

I watched him climb up the rocks to the canyon rim. At the top he waved. I didn't wave back.

Well, the next Sunday I climbed down to the ledge to find Coleman already there. So much for my private hideaway.

When he saw me coming down the rocks, he waved and motioned for me to sit next to him. When I was seated, he reached in a little cooler and handed me a soda, then took one himself. We stared at the dam and sipped the sodas.

"Been working here long?" he asked.

"Three years. Motor pool."

"I'm four years. Power plant engineer."

I would have been glad if our conversation had ended right there, but after a few minutes Coleman said, "You think the dam can stop the river?"

It seemed a dumb thing to ask. "Sure hope so. Otherwise we've been working for nothing."

He frowned. "Yeah, that's what everybody thinks, if you pour enough concrete you can stop the river. And when I look at the dam from up here I say, Yeah, it'll work. Hey, I'm an engineer, I know it's supposed to work. But when I'm down by the river I'm not so sure." He paused. "You ever been down close this time of year, when it's really moving?"

I shook my head.

He said, "Well, you get down close, and you see that there is a depth and a great power to the water. And you start to think, A dam can't stop this."

"They did it in Nevada."

He grunted. "That's the Colorado. This is the Columbia. Big difference."

He stared at the concrete mass and said, "Maybe the dam will stop the river. For a while. A short while."

Another crazy comment, I thought. "What do you mean, a short while? Concrete's tough, man. Heavy and tough. It stays. That dam will be there a long time after we're gone."

He nodded. "That's for sure. But we're not here any time at all, so that's not saying much."

I felt a bit of anger building. I said, "Well, some of us are here longer than others."

"Luke, you're talking ten years, twenty, fifty, eighty. It's nothing."

"A man's whole life is nothing? Or a girl's?"

His brow furrowed, like he was thinking about my words. "That's not what I meant. But the time we're here is so short compared to—"

"To what?"

He finished his soda and put down the bottle. "You ever walk out in the desert at night?"

"Maybe. So what?"

"I don't do that very often myself, but there are times when I do. When the wind is calm, and when there is no moon, or a nearly new moon, I go out in the desert, away from town. Now, those conditions don't happen very often at the same time. That dusty wind around here is pretty consistent, but maybe once or twice a year there will be a calm night and a new moon at the same time."

"So?"

"So, you can walk out, and you're far from the big cities, and the air is dry and cold and still, and there's no light from anywhere. And you can raise up your face and look into eternity. And when you see that eternity, that unchanging heaven, you know that the dam's life will be short. Longer than ours, yes, but not very long compared to what's up there."

I grunted. "Why think about it?"

He laughed. "That's a good question, Luke. Most folks don't think about it. I figure most of the men around here would rather be in a pool hall or beer joint than out staring at the stars. But I do think about it. It's just the way I am. Say, you know what's gonna happen to that dam in the long term?"

"Nope."

"It'll be a waterfall. You see, the river brings silt down with it. The Columbia's a clear river, not like the Mississippi, but even the Columbia carries silt. Over the years the silt builds up behind the dam. The day comes when there's no lake behind the dam anymore, just the river itself, cascading over the top of the dam. Then the river starts to eat away the concrete, and the waterfall gets a tiny bit lower every year. The day finally comes when the dam is two chunks of concrete on either side of the river. The river wins in the end. Will anyone see that? Who knows whether people, humans, will still be around then. But the river will be there, and the stars. God wants the river to flow, Luke. Our work here is very temporary."

The anger was building in me. "Maybe God doesn't care one way or another."

He turned to me. "God has purposes."

I thought, You pious know-it-all. You just ruined my Sunday afternoon.

I started to get up and leave, but in my anger I needed to say something. "Do you have a family, Bob?"

"Yep. Wife and daughter. Brought 'em here from Portland. Mason City's not the best place to raise a kid, but she does okay."

"How old?"

"Twelve."

"Did she come from God?"

Coleman stared at me. "That's a funny thing to ask."

I shook my head and looked down at the river. "Not really. You're the one that started with the God talk. I'm asking if you think your daughter came from God."

"Well, yes. When she was born, my wife and I said she was a gift from God. We still feel that way."

I held out the soda bottle. "You gave me this soda a few minutes ago. You let me keep it. It was a gift, right?"

He nodded.

"You didn't take it back, but you could have, right?"

"Why would I—"

"You could have grabbed it out of my hand and smashed it down on the rocks, couldn't you?"

"But—"

"But you're a good man, and you let me keep it." I stood. "I'm going back to town. Thanks for the soda."

I was halfway up the rocks when I turned. I had one more thing to say, and I yelled it. "I wonder if you'd talk about God so much if your daughter went to school one day and never came home."

Coleman never returned to the ledge. It was mine alone, once again. But every time I went out there, I found myself thinking about the man who, like me, could spend an afternoon looking at a dam. Part of me wished he would come back. An anger churned in me when I thought about him. I wanted to curse him.

I kept thinking about what he said, about looking at the river up close. One Sunday I left the ledge and walked downriver a few miles to an access road that led into the canyon. I went down to the river's edge and made my way over the rocks back toward the dam.

Coleman had been right. The surging power of that river couldn't be seen from up above. You had to be down close.

I watched the water roar over the temporary spillway in the

dam's center. In that white waterfall I saw fish jumping. In the water near the shore, dead fish floated, big ones.

I headed back downriver. About a mile from the dam I saw a man sitting on a boulder near the shore. I knew it was Coleman before I was even close enough to see his face.

I walked to the boulder. He turned, and smiled when he recognized me.

I said, "Thought you might come back to the ledge sometime."

"No, Luke, that's your ledge. You're a man who likes to be alone. But you know what? I like it better down here. I come down here on Sundays now."

I leaned against the rock. I didn't have anything to say, but something kept me there.

Coleman said, "You know about the salmon?"

I shrugged.

"They're trying to get upriver this time of year. Did you see them trying to jump up that spillway?"

I nodded. "Why?"

"Why? Just trying to get back where they were born, that's all. Those fish hatched up above here, maybe even up in Canada. They let the river take them to the sea when they were very small. Now they're trying to get back where they were born, so they can spawn, then die. The cycle starts and ends where they were born. But now they can't get home. Oh, they can jump a waterfall. Ten feet high, maybe even twenty feet. They jump with great power. But they can't jump that spillway. So they die right here. And they can't jump a five-hundred-foot high dam, so there'll never be salmon again upriver from here."

"How did they get this far? What about Bonneville?"

"Bonneville's got fish ladders. Why doesn't this dam? Don't ask me. Wouldn't have cost that much more to put in fish ladders."

I shrugged. "See you around." I started to walk away.

"Luke, wait."

When I stopped he said, "I've thought a lot about what you said up there on the ledge. About me grabbing that soda bottle back. And I've thought about that last thing you yelled down from the rocks. I want to ask you, did someone not come home to you one time? I'd like to know."

I wanted to crack a fist into his face. I wanted to put my hands around his neck and squeeze with all my strength, until his face turned purple, and his eyes bulged out. But I didn't do that. I cursed him loudly, then turned and walked away. I never went down to the river again, and never again set eyes on Bob Coleman.

I was proud of my curse. I got in a bunch of words from the church and a bunch of words from the pool hall, and I mixed 'em together real nice. I knew it was a curse Coleman wouldn't quickly forget. He might even remember it when he looked up at the stars.

Even in winter, when the days were short, overcast, and cold, I went to the ledge on Sundays. In fog, mist, or snow I went to the ledge. Habit ruled me.

Six months after the last encounter with Coleman, I sat on the ledge one Sunday and looked through falling snow at a dam almost completed. Five hundred fifty feet above the river and a mile across the canyon. The biggest man-made structure on earth.

Some work remained. The two power plants were still unfinished. But the laborers had already started to leave, and I knew that in a few months there would no longer be a motor pool at Grand Coulee. I'd have to move on.

But to where? Finding a job wouldn't be a problem, thanks to Hitler. I read the papers. I knew that industry was revving up. I could find work, but never an environment that suited me as perfectly as Grand Coulee, the desolate dump of a town with its army of working men. I had become one with the desert. Tex, the nameless loner, without friends or family. Just the way I wanted it.

I still couldn't help thinking about the past now and then. Daydreams are sometimes hard to push away, just like night dreams. As I watched those snowflakes drift down, I remembered another snowfall. Sis had woke me up, excited. She had never seen snow before. Later that morning I promised her and Mom a telephone. Sis came around the table to hug me. I remember her hug giving me joy, but I couldn't remember what joy felt like.

The sky began to darken for the long night, so I climbed up the rocks and headed back to town. I walked into the dormitory and found it buzzing. Men stood around in groups, talking loudly. I went up to a fellow standing by himself and asked what all the excitement was about.

He looked surprised. "Where have you been, man? You didn't hear the Japs bombed our fleet in Hawaii? We're in a war, Mister!"

26

Russ

Sunday morning, final hymn, third stanza of "Have Thine Own Way, Lord." A woman whose face I didn't notice walked down the left aisle toward the back of the church. I didn't think anything of it, sang the first two lines of the last stanza, and eased out of the pew headed for the back door, my usual routine to avoid the post-service chatter and fellowship.

She was waiting at the bottom of the steps, and her stare made it clear that I was not going to get past her. I came to an awkward stop—the routine of many years is not easily modified—and greeted her with "Miss Orr" in as pleasant a voice as I could muster. She wore a gray dress with gathered short sleeves, and a small white hat was perched on top of her dark hair.

"Oh you *do* know my last name." Her tone was friendly, but I sensed irony. I nodded.

She frowned. "That door's going to open in a minute, and we're in the way. Let's go over there." I followed her to a corner of the building. She turned and said, "I need to talk to you."

I made a feeble attempt to end things. "Well, I have a guest at home, and I need to go fix dinner."

Her reply was lightning quick. "Oh, I think your guest can wait a few minutes for his dinner." Briefly, fire and ice in two pretty blue eyes.

I gave in and smiled with a shrug. "All right."

"Please call me Vicky. May I call you Russ?"

I nodded.

"Well, Russ, you and I have been going to this church for quite some time now."

"Yes."

"I remember when you joined, about ... eight years ago, right?"

"I reckon."

"But I don't know you. Nor does anyone else. You come at the last minute and sit on the back pew. You leave before the benediction. You never come to other church functions. In fact, I might never have been aware of you at all if it weren't for one thing."

I could feel my heart beat faster. Where was she going with this?

"That one thing is your voice. During the hymns your voice comes through the other voices. Oh, you try to blend. You're not louder than the others, just clearer, richer. You can't hide that voice, Russ. Why aren't you in the choir?"

I shrugged. "Guess I'm a loner."

She nodded. "I can understand that. You're a loner and a man of habit. Back pew, leave during last hymn. I know about habit. I've sat on that third pew for the last ten years."

She gazed into the distance, silent for a few moments, then said. "Everyone's left. Let's go in the sanctuary and sit. Get out of the sun." I followed her up the steps past the lingering worshippers. She sat on the rear pew and motioned me to sit beside her.

She locked onto my eyes. "Russ, where did you live before you moved here?"

I fidgeted. I smoothed my eyebrow with a finger. I looked at my watch.

She said, "All right, forget it. I'm a snoop and a busybody. Somebody else called me that one time. I don't really need to know about you. But, I do have a question or two about your … guest, if you don't mind."

I nodded slowly.

"I'm sure you're aware that I know him, from my visit to the yard in Henderson. You probably overheard a bit of that conversation, huh?"

The changing hue of my face answered her question.

"Yes, Russ, I knew Luke before it happened. You probably think we dated. Hah. Dated. What a joke." She gave a sarcastic giggle.

"You know what? We actually did have a date one time. Met in a garage, and he drove me out to his drilling rig. He laughed with me. He even touched me—actually put his hand on my wrist and caressed my arm. But he didn't kiss me. Oh, no. Maybe I should have kissed him. Pretty bold for a 'nice' girl, huh? But maybe I should have. I think about that a lot. After that afternoon, nothing. He went out with these floozies up in Kilgore, these chain-smoking rum-guzzlers with overdone makeup. But I went two other places with him. I went to Overton with him one night, to the Legion hall, and two days later I went to church with him."

Her voice had risen with her last words. She laid her face in her hands and sobbed.

I took a handkerchief from my suit pocket and handed it to her. Her tears bothered me. I wanted her to stop. I said, "He appreciated you sitting with him at the funeral."

Her hands dropped from her face, and her wide wet eyes drilled into me. "He *told* you that?"

"Yes."

Her brow furrowed. "What all *did* he tell you, Russ?"

"A lot. Pretty much his whole life, I guess. He likes to talk when we're working together outdoors."

She repositioned herself on the pew, and I knew we wouldn't be leaving anytime soon.

"Did he tell you that I was the one who brought him the word about Marty?"

"Yes."

"Did he tell you he cursed me?"

I nodded.

She swallowed, and I thought the tears might come back, but her voice was firm. "I remember the words of his curse. I have remembered them every day of my life for the last ten years."

"Well, he knew why you had come. He wasn't cursing you. He was cursing something, someone, else."

"I know what you're saying. But the words of a curse have a power, Russ. A staying power. I just can't help but feel that he … hates me for bringing him the word about his sister."

I shook my head. "Don't think so."

"You said he's telling you his life story. Why?"

I thought for a second, then said, "I think he's been alone for ten years. Hasn't talked to anyone, shared anything with anyone. His story, and his sister's story, were all bottled up inside him. It was like a … pressure. He had to let it out. Working with me gave him a chance to do that."

"Had to tell it to another man."

"Yes."

"Couldn't have told it to a woman."

"Don't think so."

She nodded and gazed at the floor for a moment.

"Russ, why did he come back? He came a long, long way. Why?"

"I don't know. I've wondered the same thing. Acts like he's going back to where he came from pretty soon."

She stared straight ahead, silent. A minute or so passed, and when she finally spoke her voice was low and soft. "Yes, he will soon move on. I am thirty-three years old. A fine man asked me to marry him, a chemist. Worked for an oil company. I turned him down. Then I met another man, an engineer for the highway department, and he asked me. I stalled, and he finally gave up. They both have their own families now. I teach children for a year, then they move on, and I teach other children. Everyone moves on. Everyone but me."

She rose. "Thank you for talking to me. I'm sure Luke is getting hungry." She held out her hand, and I took it as I stood. She picked up her purse from the pew and walked toward the back door. I followed. At the steps she turned to me and said, "I heard a song a few years ago. I liked it. It seemed to be about me. It's called 'I'm Waiting for Ships That Never Come In.'"

She reached in her purse for keys and walked toward her car, but turned to me and said, "Russ, you really should join the choir. Don't hide that beautiful voice." One final wave and she was gone.

27

Luke

War. We had all seen it coming, we thought, but when it got here we were a little shocked. Not for long though.

A lot of the younger fellows at the dam joined up right away. I thought about doing that, but my boss asked me to stay at least another couple of months, since I was the senior engine mechanic. During that time I learned about the need for experienced workers in the defense industry. People told me I that with my skills I could contribute to the war effort better as a defense worker than as a soldier or sailor.

We started to hear about job openings in Seattle. They built ships in Seattle, and there was a big aircraft factory there, too. In mid-February a couple of other mechanics and I took a train to Seattle. I hired on as an apprentice shipfitter, building a destroyer in the Puget Sound shipyard. I learned the job quickly and finished my apprenticeship in two months. The Navy needed the ship soon, and we worked seven days a week. But we didn't complain, knowing of the younger men out on the sea, risking their lives, losing their lives.

The war gave my life a purpose. The work exhausted me. Sleep, breakfast, work, dinner, work, supper, sleep. I grew into the routine.

◆ ◆ ◆

The ship came together, and we looked with pride on our work, anxious to finish so the ship could go into battle. But I wanted to finish for another reason. After fifteen months, I despised the rain and fog and crowds of Seattle. I longed for the dryness and loneliness of the desert. I wanted to move on, and the completion of the ship seemed to me a sign that I should do so. But how could I go back to the desert? The dam was finished.

I had almost resigned myself to staying on at the shipyard when I saw the flier in the union hall one day.

Men Wanted

Bricklayers

Pipefitters

Welders

Heavy Equipment Operators

Carpenters

Laborers

Critical War-Related Work

Report to E. I. DuPont de Nemours Co.

Richland, Washington

I'd never heard of Richland. I asked around and learned it was a little north of Kennewick, where I'd crossed the big river on my way to Grand Coulee years earlier. Now I could go back to the desert. I rode a train east the next day.

Russ, I got what I wanted. Back in the desert, back in a ramshackle town with thousands of other men, working in the dust and the heat and the cold, building something.

There was a big difference though. At the dam I knew what I worked on. I could watch the concrete being poured and see the dam grow. I could imagine what the finished dam would look like, and could understand how the falling water could make turbines spin and create power. I could visualize how the dammed-up water could be diverted to irrigate crops and turn scrubland into farm-land. A man can take pride in his work when he understands the purpose.

In Richland I did not have that understanding. And I learned early on—don't ask. Don't ask what it is, don't ask what it's gonna do. Don't ask why it's out here in the desert and the dust, rather than closer to a city where men could live with their families. Don't ask about all the soldiers with machine guns. Don't ask about all the pipes for the river water, or why anything, any process, would need so much water. Don't ask why so much concrete. Don't ask why there's such a hurry to get everything done, or what it has to do with the war.

Don't ask, don't tell strangers what you're doing, and keep the guesses inside your head. I didn't have any trouble following those orders, but I still longed for the clarity of building a dam.

They called it the Hanford Engineer Works. The government owned all the land—about eight hundred square miles, I heard. Buildings and plants were going up by the dozens. They had to build a new town to house the workers.

Richland. Windy, dusty, rough. A lot like Grand Coulee, but much bigger. Every once in a while I'd hear "Hey, Tex!" Lots of for-mer dam workers came to Hanford, like me.

I worked as a pipefitter, seven days a week, which suited me fine. I knew that what we were building must be critical to the war. Sometimes lying in my bunk waiting for sleep I'd try to guess the purpose of the big project.

What about the three strange buildings near the river? I had worked on the pipework for the exteriors, but I never saw the insides. You had to have a badge to go inside, and most of us didn't have badges. But the water pipes going into the building were huge. The water was pumped out of the river into purification plants, then pumped to the three buildings, then back to the river. I figured it had to be some kind of heat exchange, but not the usual process where water is heated to become steam and furnish power. No, here the heated water was returned to the river.

Something, some process, was hot and needed to be cooled. But why so much water, and why the concrete-lined deep pools at the ends of all three buildings? And why did the water need to be purified if it was simply being used as a coolant?

Those buildings were strange, but the new ones behind Gable Mountain were stranger. People called them the "Queen Marys." They were as big as ships. Except for a few doors at ground level, they looked like solid blocks of concrete, eight hundred feet long and eighty feet high.

One time in the mess hall I overheard a man say that the concrete walls on those buildings were seven feet thick. That sounded to me like something designed to take a direct bomb hit. But whose bomb? We knew that the Jap navy was crumbling and in no shape to attack the U.S. mainland. Besides, Jap planes would be shot down long before they reached central Washington.

One night I had a thought. The thick concrete was not to protect what was inside, it was to keep what was inside from getting out. I decided the U.S. was testing poison gas inside the Queen Marys, gas that would be used when we invaded Japan. I kept the guess to myself.

◆ ◆ ◆

Whatever its purpose, the complex was finally complete, and operational. Most of the construction men were laid off and went on to other jobs, happy to leave the dust and desolation. I stayed, as a maintenance worker.

I remember a spring day when our crew was laying a pipeline a mile north of Gable Mountain. All of a sudden one of the men yelled and pointed south. A huge plume of brown smoke drifted over the mountain, toward us. Had there been an explosion? Did one of the Queen Marys lie in ruins? Was poison gas now drifting in our direction?

I sensed the fear of my coworkers. I remembered a white cloud of mortar dust, rising over pine trees. I had felt great fear then, fear for Marty. But I didn't fear the brown cloud, for it threatened nothing of value to me.

A government truck braked to a stop beside us, and the badge-wearing driver told us not to worry. All part of the process, he said. He sped off, churning up gray dust. We went back to work. I thought, What has a man become when he doesn't fear anything?

Spring became summer. The rains went away, as usual, and the desert baked, as usual. The "process" continued. The men with the badges seemed to be satisfied, almost relaxed, as they went about their business. To those of us with the incomplete knowledge, it became clear that the "process" worked.

We were finishing breakfast in the mess hall on a Monday morning in early August. We heard a shout and looked up to see a government man holding a radio. "Big news!" he yelled, and motioned with his arm. He went over to the reading area and plugged in the radio. We got up and gathered around while the tubes warmed. The government man said, "War's gonna be over soon, guys."

I can't remember everything I heard that morning. So much, and so unbelievable. One of our B-29s had dropped a special bomb on Hiroshima, Japan. It had gone off like twenty thousand tons of TNT. It had wiped out the city.

They had developed it at Los Alamos, New Mexico, in secrecy. Had tested it just three weeks earlier. Called it the atomic bomb. But some folks called it the sun bomb, because when it went off, it was brighter than the sun.

Amazing, but the real surprise came next. The Hanford Engineer Works—the hundreds of buildings, the Queen Marys, everything—had been built for the sole reason of making the special "fuel" for the bomb. Plutonium, they called it. We heard about another big complex called Oak Ridge, in Tennessee. They made uranium, and we made plutonium, both fuels for the sun bomb.

We were told we could take the morning off, so we could hear more news. I walked out to the river to think about what I'd heard.

I doubted that the bomb would end the war. Not after what happened in the Pacific, on the islands. The Japanese had been defeated there. But they never surrendered. They stayed in their bunkers and caves and fought, and our troops had to go in with tanks and flame-throwers and grenades and find every cave and every bunker and destroy them. Island after island, the same story.

Something about what I'd heard on the radio bothered me, but I couldn't pin it down. I tried to remember the highlights.

"… twenty thousand tons of TNT …"

"… brighter than the sun …"

"… night became day in the desert of New Mexico …"

"… extreme measure of using the bomb …"

"… three new cities built to house the workers and their families …"

I found that certain words had a weight in my mind.

"… three new cities … workers and their families …"

"… cities … families …"

"… city of Hiroshima at eight sixteen Monday morning Hiroshima time …"

Then I realized the word that carried the heaviest weight: "*City.*" I turned to look at the town of Richland. An anger came alive inside me.

They dropped it on a city.

I walked away from the fast-flowing blue water, back toward the plant, the Hanford Engineer Works. My mind boiled with a single thought.

They dropped it on a city. I helped make the fuel for the sun bomb, and they dropped it on a city.

◆ ◆ ◆

Three days later, it happened again. Another city, Nagasaki.

A hatred rose up in me, against my own country. Why didn't they drop the bombs on the naval yards? Kill sailors, not women. Destroy warships, not homes.

Was I the only one to feel that way? I decided to go to a bar and have a few drinks and listen to the conversations around me.

I went into town and found a crowded tavern. I headed toward an empty bar stool, but then heard, "Hey, Tex!"

Andy, a welder I'd worked with a few times, pointed to an empty chair at his table. I wished I'd gone to a different tavern, but I walked over and sat down next to Andy. He introduced his two drinking buddies, and I ordered a beer from the waitress.

"What do you think, Tex? Think they'll surrender now?" Andy asked.

All three of them looked at me. This wasn't what I wanted. I needed to listen, not talk. Where was that beer?

I glanced toward the bar, then turned back and stared at the table top. "No, I don't think they'll surrender. If the first one didn't make 'em do it, the second one won't make any difference."

The red-headed stocky man next to Andy nodded his head. "That's what I've been saying, but these two think otherwise."

The waitress set the beer down, and I paid her, pulled the bottle to my lips, and took a long swallow.

The fourth man spoke. "Yeah. See, the first bomb might have been one-of-a-kind, that's what the Japs probably thought. But yesterday they found out different. Where there's two, there could be three, four, ten, enough to wipe out the whole island. I say they'll give up."

"Wonder how many there really are. How many of those bombs we got?" Andy asked.

The fourth man said, "I hope we got a hundred of 'em. And I hope we use 'em, and wipe out every city on that godforsaken island."

We drank in silence. I motioned the waitress for another beer. "I've been wondering something." No one replied. I spoke louder.

"I've been wondering … in Japan, do they have school in August?"

They stared at me, and I took another long swallow.

"Who cares, Mister?" said the fourth man.

"Yeah, Tex, that's a crazy thing to ask," Andy said.

I fingered the top of the bottle, then opened my hands in a shrug. "I guess it is, Andy. But, see, if they have school in August, then the kids were probably in school yesterday when it happened. It was about eleven in the morning, I heard." I found myself breathing faster.

"I guess what I'm saying is, when a school gets blown up, and the boys and girls get killed, that should be an accident. You shouldn't do that on purpose. You shouldn't blow up schools on purpose."

The fourth man's sharp, booming voice silenced all conversation in the room, and heads turned toward the man. "I'll tell you something else you shouldn't do, Mister. You shouldn't send your planes to bomb Pearl Harbor and kill two thousand men and start a war!"

My reply was low and soft, but in the quiet of the room every-one heard it. "They bombed the ships and the airfields. They didn't bomb Honolulu."

The fourth man's chair scraped against the wood floor as he pushed back from the table and stood, a tall fellow with a square face, jutting jaw, and thick black hair. His chest heaved. Andy and the red-headed man got up and edged toward the bar.

I took another swig and waited.

He growled, "My kid brother died on Peleliu. They shot him from their cave. He didn't have a chance. Stand up, Jap lover."

I pushed back my chair and stepped up to face him. "I'm sorry about your brother, but you don't call me names." I made a fist and raised it. He swung, and everything went dark.

I woke up to dust, dried blood, an eye swollen shut, and white-hot pain. I lay in the dirt just outside the tavern, next to a parked car. My head rested on a towel. A middle-aged woman gently pressed a wet dishtowel to my face. I moaned, and the woman spoke.

"You just shouldn't have said those things, Mister. Not in there, not tonight."

I sat up and touched my swollen face. "How long have I been here?"

"About an hour. They drug you out here. The cops came, but when they heard you started it, they left. I've been trying to clean you up a little. You might have a broken nose, you better go to a doctor."

"Why are you helping me?"

She lowered her eyes. "My husband owns the bar. I heard what you said. I think you're right. I think they were wrong to drop those bombs on the cities. But you can't say that right now, you just can't say that."

The woman stood and helped me up. I thanked her and started to walk away.

She said, "Hey, Mister, why didn't you fight that guy? You're a big man, you could have got in a lick or two."

I turned to her. "His little brother died in the war. I felt real sorry for that fellow. I couldn't hit him."

28

Russ

We finished up the second rock garden on Friday afternoon, and it had to be the hottest day of the summer. The lady whose yard we worked in brought us some cold lemonade in mid-afternoon and told us the temperature was one hundred two degrees. We were real happy to finish up that job around six-thirty and head home.

I followed my usual routine when we got to the house, which was to go check the mailbox. I don't get much mail, so I was surprised to see three letters sitting there. One of them said AIR MAIL on the envelope, and had a stamp with a picture of an airplane. Now who would send me an air mail letter?

But it wasn't my letter. It was addressed to Luke Robertson, care of me. Postmarked San Diego.

The next letter was mine, and I recognized my oldest son's handwriting. The third letter didn't have a stamp, and it wasn't sealed. I opened it right away. It was a note from a pastor of a church in Henderson, offering me the job of landscaping the church ground. The church folks had seen our work around town and wanted a similar treatment for their churchyard.

I went inside and handed Luke his letter, and he read his while I read mine. I decided it was too hot to cook and made us some big ham sandwiches for supper. When we were ready to eat, Luke brought his letter to the table, handed it to me and told me to read it.

Dear Luke,

I got Vicky's telegram yesterday.

When I read it, I started to cry. My five-year-old saw me and said, "What's wrong, Mommy?" I told her, "Luke is alive." And she said, "But Mommy, isn't that good?" I laughed through my tears.

I need to back up a little. You see, when my little girl was just learning to talk, we would say a little prayer together at night, just before she went to bed. It was just me and her; my husband Seth was in the Pacific. Anyway, we always gave thanks for everything, and we prayed for her daddy, but the last words we said in that prayer were "God be with Luke." Yes, I told my little girl about you, and that you were gone, and we didn't know where, but we wanted God to be with you. And she said those words even before she knew what they meant.

I cried when I read the letter, and I told her my tears were tears of joy. She already knew about tears of joy because Seth and I cried our eyes out when he finally came home after the war, and we were delirious with happiness.

But a few hours after I read that letter, something happened. I felt this huge anger boiling up inside of me, and it grew, and I cursed you, Luke. I cursed you with words you wouldn't think I knew. And the thought of what you did to me made me hate you.

I needed you so bad in those days after it happened. I needed you to put your arms around me and lift me up and hold me like you did when you swung me out over the pond.

I needed you to comfort me. Yes, I know that when you looked at me, you thought of Marty because we were always together. Well, it was the same with me. When I looked at you, I thought of Marty, and it hurt. But I could stand that hurt. What I couldn't stand was the hurt of you leaving, and not saying good-bye, and not ever contacting us.

You were like a big brother to me, and you left, and the more I thought about it after I got the letter, the more angry I got. The anger took over me. I started getting angry with Becky, and Jimmy, and Seth. I was being eaten up with anger.

This morning though, I let my mind go back, back to the days before it happened. I thought about how much you and Marty loved each other. I said to myself, I can't blame him. He was hurting more than I can know, and I can't blame him. I said the words out loud: I forgive you, Luke. And the second I said those words, I felt this indescribable joy come into my heart, and it pushed out all the anger and hate. Every bit of it. And I cried again, tears of joy.

Luke, I do forgive you, and I'll pray for you just like I always have. I don't know when we'll see each other, but you will be in my thoughts and prayers every day.

There's one other thing I want to tell you. When I had my little girl, we thought about naming her Marty. But I can't mix the memories. I can't mix any other memory with the memory of Marty.

I love you, Luke

Rie

I handed the letter back. Luke said, "Sis would have made a good mother. She'd be twenty-three right now. I might have a niece or a nephew."

While we ate the sandwiches I told him about my letters. "Luke, my son's invited me to visit. Wants me to come next Saturday. Now, I just got another landscaping job. Church in Henderson. Working together we can finish in four or five days. On Saturday morning we can drive to the train station in Longview. I'll head for Dallas, and you can go wherever you want. What do you say?"

He nodded. "Sounds good."

I knew he wasn't quite through with his story.

We rested Saturday. It was too hot to go outside. We just sat around and let the fan blow on us.

Sunday cooled off a bit, upper nineties. I worked in the garden that afternoon, but had to take rest breaks about every half-hour due to the heat. During one of those breaks I was sitting on the back porch when I heard a female voice. "Anybody home?"

I heard Luke walk to the door and say, "Hello again, Vicky."

"May I come in? I brought something."

I heard the screen door open. Vicky said, "It's a chocolate pie, for you and Russ."

A brief silence, then footsteps. Vicky asked, "Can we talk a minute?" I heard them pull out the chairs and sit.

She said, "I'm glad you didn't leave when you said."

"Here 'til Saturday. Helping the old man with one last job. Then we're both leaving. He's going to visit his son, and I'm heading back to Seattle."

"Where is Russ now?"

"In the garden."

"All right. Well, the reason I'm here is, I got a letter from Rie, and in the letter she told me how she forgave you, and when she did, she felt great joy and peace. I have been in a lot of turmoil since I talked to you, and I realize it's because there's still a resentment at what you did. In church this morning I made a decision, to forgive you, just like Rie did. And I'm asking your forgiveness for the way I talked to you before."

Luke said, "Doesn't matter. You didn't say anything I didn't deserve. You don't need my forgiveness."

"I'll decide what I need, thank you. And I'm asking you to forgive me. Do you?" Her voice had a little edge to it.

"Okay, sure. Doesn't mean a thing."

"I wish you weren't leaving."

"Don't know why you'd say that."

"I'd like to talk to you, and hear what you've been doing all these years."

"You want to know? I'll tell you one thing. I worked on the atom bomb. You know, the one that blew up all the kids and women. Yeah, plutonium man, that's me. We made the plutonium. That was the Nagasaki bomb. You don't want to know about me, Vicky. You don't want to know where I've been, and who I've been with. You're a decent woman. And if you'd bring pies to decent men instead of bums, maybe you'd be married by now."

Silence. My curiosity fought my better judgment and won. I leaned over and peeked through the back door. Vicky stood in front of Luke holding the pie with both hands.

Her words dropped like sleet from a dark cloud. "All right, Luke. I'll go find a decent man. But I made this pie for you, and you're going to have it."

Splat. Right in the face, with good aim. White meringue, dark brown filling, tan crust, all now merged with black hair and beard.

She pulled the pan away and walked out the front door. But seconds later she marched back in, put her face six inches from his right ear and screamed, "You didn't kill her! Stop wallowing in it!"

She ran to her car and drove away.

A half-hour later Luke had scrubbed most of the pie out of his hair and beard. His only comment was, "Stupid woman. That was a real good-tasting pie. Why'd she waste it like that?"

29

Luke

Those bombs took it out of me, Russ. I must have been alone in feeling the way I did. I remember VJ day and the celebrations in the streets, the joy on the faces, the relief that the war was over. People said that the bombs did it, the bombs ended the war. But I kept visualizing those huge sun-balls and the people beneath them. Women, old men, children. Not soldiers. Seventy-eight thousand dead in Hiroshima alone. And I had worked seven days a week to make it possible.

The dam and the war had given me reasons to live. Now I had nothing. I despised the men who made that bomb, and the men who dropped it.

I was finished with Hanford, forever. Didn't even bother to pick up my last paycheck. I headed south to Kennewick, crossed the river to Pasco, and found the Northern Pacific rail yard. I found the eastbound departure tracks, waited 'til nightfall, and climbed in a boxcar. Spokane was my destination. Nobody knew me there.

I got to Spokane and found a cheap downtown hotel with weekly rates. I paid for six months in advance. I had saved money during the work years and figured I could exist for a long time on it.

For eighteen months I wandered the streets of Spokane. At first I spent a lot of time at the railroad station. There were some benches out on the platforms, and I'd sit there for hours at a time and watch the passenger trains come in. The trains brought the soldiers and sailors and Marines home.

Wives and children and parents and brothers and sisters would come to meet the trains. The men would step down from the trains in their uniforms. The families would greet them with hugs that seemed to last forever, and tears.

I sometimes wished I could talk to those men. Soldier, you fought the Germans. You brought down Hitler. You freed Europe. Well done, Soldier, I would have said.

Sailor, you went against the Japanese fleet. Those were dangerous waters, far from home. But you pounded the enemy, and wasted his ships. Well done, Sailor.

Marine, you took the islands, those pits of hell with their caves and bunkers and desperate men who would never surrender. You're a brave man, Marine.

You fought well, I wanted to tell those men. That's war. You killed other soldiers and sailors, not women, not children. You destroyed tanks and planes and ships, not cities.

I went to that train station and sat on the same bench every day for about three months. Then one morning a cop touched me on the shoulder with a nightstick and said, "No loitering. Move on."

I wondered why he picked on me. Other folks sat on the benches. Then I felt my face and realized I hadn't shaved in a week.

What did I do after that, for the next fifteen months? Nothing. I stayed in my room, or walked up and down the streets. I ate, drank, slept. In winter I waited for spring. In summer I waited for fall.

Last spring I decided to go to Seattle. I'm not sure why, or what I expected to find there. I drifted west on the freight trains. I found a flophouse near the shipyard. I needed to touch a woman. I found women to touch, and paid them. I could get what I needed, and didn't have to talk to 'em, as long as I paid them.

Then one night I remembered sitting at the supper table with Mom and Sis. We had talked about the beach pajama ladies in Kilgore. I told Sis the ladies let men they don't know kiss them and stuff, for money. I remember Mom's anger that I would even joke about it with Sis. What would Mom think of me now? What would Sis think?

I really didn't have much reason for being alive, and I got to thinking: How long can a man without a reason for living stay around? Nah, I didn't think about killing myself. Suicide didn't appeal to me. I didn't long for death. I didn't long for anything. And when a man doesn't long for anything, what's to keep him going?

I decided to go talk it over with Sis. She's not a little girl anymore, I thought. She's twenty-three years old. That's close to the age I was when I last saw her. So she has seen right and wrong, and good and evil. Maybe she can tell me what to do. I thought: I'll go to her grave, like I did so many times before. And I'll stay there until I know what to do.

It was a crazy thought, but for a man with nothing, even a crazy thought can have a pull.

That night before I went to sleep, another thought came to me: The salmon swim home to die. That's what Bob Coleman told me. And he must have been smart, he said he could see eternity. I went to sleep satisfied with the rightness of my decision.

◆ ◆ ◆

My money had just about run out, but the freight trains were free. On a bright June morning I walked to the Union Pacific yard, and at noon a train pulled my boxcar south. Portland, that night, brought a choice. Stay with the UP, or jump over to the Southern

Pacific and reverse my northbound journey of ten years earlier. I decided to stay with the UP. I had seen enough of California and its Okie-haters.

A couple of days later I made it to Salt Lake. I hopped over to the Denver and Rio Grande Western to head for Denver. I almost didn't get there.

It was early afternoon, two days beyond Salt Lake. I lay in the back of the boxcar, my head on my canvas bag, my eyes closed. All of a sudden the train noise got louder and seemed to echo. I opened my eyes to darkness. Tunnel. I'd been through them before.

After a half-minute or so I started to breathe smoke, and cough. I hoped the tunnel would end. Then I remembered something.

Hobo camp, somewhere on the Southern Pacific in Oregon, ten years in the past. Around the fire, the stories of riding the rails. And the white-whiskered old-timer had told us, if you're going east, take the UP through Wyoming. Don't try to cross the Rockies on the Rio Grande. If you do, make sure it's the Tennessee Pass line, not the Moffat line. Don't ride through the Moffat. You might not make it. That's what the old-timer had said. And I remembered someone asking why not, and I remembered the answer.

The Moffat Tunnel is six and a half miles long, the old-timer had said.

I reached in the canvas bag for my spare shirt and put it over my mouth and nose.

Five minutes later the shirt was saturated with soot. I coughed with every breath, and my lungs burned. I crawled to a corner of the boxcar and put my face to the walls. I breathed in smoke and coughed.

The minutes passed. Blackness, and hot smoke and soot filling my nose and mouth and lungs. I felt fear and anger. This was not my plan. I didn't want to die on a freight train.

I fought to stay conscious. I banged my fists bloody against the walls of the boxcar, and coughed up solid particles.

I had just about given up when I saw, dimly, the rock wall of the tunnel through the boxcar door. I crawled on my belly to the door and stuck out my head and looked east, and through soot-filled eyes I could see a sliver of brightness. Moments later the gray of the tunnel wall turned into the dark green of mountain forests, and I sucked cold cedar-scented air into my starved lungs.

I spent two days in Denver recovering from that experience. But surviving it only proved the rightness of my plan.

It took me ten more days to get to Longview. Rode on four different railroads after Denver. When I got to Longview I spent the night in a boxcar on a siding, then started walking south the next day. At dusk I got to Pleasant Hill. I went to Sis's grave. I sat. I looked at that headstone, and in the fading light I saw the name: Martha Lee Robertson. I thought: Who knows her story besides me? Is Rie still alive? Rachel? Then it came to me, the one more thing that I needed to do. I needed to tell someone her story.

Right then I heard a voice behind me. You said, "Evenin'."

So now you know why I've been talking so much, Russ. Who knows what'll happen to me in Seattle? But you know the story. Someone besides me knows. I can leave in peace.

30

Russi

I packed my bag on Saturday morning, and we drove to the Longview train station. After we parked, I pulled out my wallet and handed Luke seventy dollars.

I said, "Haven't got paid yet for all the jobs we did. When you get to where you're going, send me your address, and I'll mail you the rest."

He took the money and nodded.

I said, "You got enough to buy a train ticket now. You don't really want to get back in a boxcar, do you?"

"I'll save the money for Seattle."

"You gonna ride through the Moffat Tunnel again?"

He smiled. "Nah. North from Denver to Cheyenne, catch a UP westbound to Salt Lake."

I handed him the key to the truck. "Use the truck if you need to. Just bring it back here and leave the key in the glove compartment. I'll take my spare key."

He took the key. Then he said, "You never did answer my question, Pastor."

"You're not the only one with a question or two."

We sat for a while longer, but I couldn't think of anything more to say, so I went in the depot to buy my ticket. The train wheezed into the station.

Luke picked up my bag and carried it to the coach. We shook hands. He thanked me for the meals and the work. I wished him good luck, and told him I looked forward to his letter.

I got a window seat on the depot side and waved to Luke as the train pulled out. He waved back.

About ten minutes later the realization sunk in that I'd never see him again. I'd only known him for three and a half weeks, but I knew him better than I knew my own sons. I thought about him getting in a boxcar and leaving the place where he was born and raised to go live far away. A deep sadness washed over me as the train rolled west.

I spent a whole month in Dallas. Two weeks with my oldest son and a week each with my youngest son and my daughter. It was good to see them all, and get caught up on the grandkids. I often thought about Luke and his story. I found myself wondering: Where is he now? Denver? Cheyenne? Salt Lake? Portland? Is he getting enough to eat?

Near the end of the visit I felt the need to get back home. I wanted to go out to Pleasant Hill and visit some graves. I wanted to go to Wilma's grave, and to Avis's, and Darla's and Annie's and Neil's, and to Marty's. Names that meant nothing to me before, but now I knew those people, thanks to Luke.

The train got me back to Longview about four o'clock on a mid-September afternoon. I found the truck in the parking lot. I tossed my bag in back, stepped in, and cranked the engine. It caught with a purr.

My mouth dropped. *My* engine did not purr. My engine clanged and coughed and pinged and rattled and wheezed.

I stepped out and looked at the truck. The familiar dents and scrapes proved it was mine. The engine purred with a beckoning softness.

I got in and drove out of the parking lot. No pinging when I let out the clutch. No clanging when I shifted gears. No roar when I cruised in third. Just a purr.

I drove home and opened the hood. The engine looked new. I checked the glove compartment for a note. Nothing.

I went inside the house and looked around. Something didn't seem right. I walked around the kitchen and the sitting room. When you live in a house a long time, you know how you leave it. I couldn't pin down exactly what was different, but some things were not where I had left them.

I was tired from the train ride and the drive, so I lay down on the couch for a nap. The closing of a car door woke me. I got up and looked through the screen. A pickup truck was just pulling away, and a man stood in my driveway. He didn't look familiar. He walked toward me. My eyes bulged. I remembered the picture of the clean-shaven man standing next to the girl and the biplane.

He stepped up on the porch and grinned. "Hi, Russ."

No beard. Black hair trimmed and combed. His pants and shirt had a few grease and oil stains, but they were a working man's clothes, not a bum's. His eyes were bright with life.

I stared at him and finally said, "You didn't leave?"

"Old man, you listened to me talk for three and a half weeks. But I'm sorry to say you're gonna have to listen some more. First, let me tell you that I've been living here in your house ever since you left. I didn't have a chance to ask your permission, but I figured you'd have said yes.

"And I put a new short block in your truck. Got tired of listening to that pinging, clattering piece of junk. I'm working for Dewey at the garage. Remember him, that mechanic from my boyhood in Overton? He owns the garage now.

"I'm gonna cook you supper tonight, Russ. You're my guest. We'll have a quiet meal, like you want. But after we eat, I'm gonna tell you the story of what happened to me after you left. Part of it I couldn't figure out how to tell. I've been thinking about how to tell you that part for the last three weeks. I think I know, now."

31

Luke

I sat there in the truck for a long time after your train pulled away. I had every intention of walking down to the switching yard and waiting for a westbound freight to stop for a crew change. I could be back in Seattle in three weeks. Out of this heat. Back where the winds off the ocean blow cool.

For some reason I got to thinking about the night we met. All the things you said to me. And one thing stuck in my mind: "It's *Marty* on the monument."

I remembered Vicky talking about the monument, too. I decided to go look at it. Wouldn't take but an hour or so, then I could come back and catch the freight.

I drove down through Kilgore to New London and parked at the little drug store. I walked across the street and stepped under the granite arms. I found her name among the seventh-graders. I found Avis and Darla and Annie's names. I found Neil's name, and Tim Halley's.

I had seen enough. I went back to the truck and drove away. But I didn't go back north on 42. I turned onto a familiar road.

The houses seemed smaller, and I realized it was because the trees had grown in the ten years since I left. I slowed, and looked at the house with the swing on the front porch, the porch I had built with my own hands. A boy and a girl sat in the swing, and looked toward me as I passed. I turned left, then left again, and passed another familiar house, and wondered if Tom and Rachel still lived there.

I turned right to drive past one more house, and heard a sound coming from that house that gave me a cold chill. Piano music. A clear, bright melody, played by someone … trained.

I needed an explanation, and so I drove to where I might find one.

◆ ◆ ◆

The red-, blue-, and white-striped pole stood by the door, unchanged. Through the front window I saw no customers, only the lone barber in his chair reading a newspaper. His hair was now gray and thinning, and his face seemed less round, more angular, more shadowed.

I opened the door, and he looked up. His eyebrows rose. "Luke!"

"Hi, Al."

"This is wonderful." He stood, and we shook hands. "I heard you were around, and I was so hoping you'd stop in. Oh, it's good to see you."

"Good to see you, Al. What happened to Pete?"

"Oh, he left early. We don't have much business late Saturday afternoon. Seems like everybody wants to go to the barber on Saturday morning. Hey, I bet you came in for a haircut and a shave. Have a seat."

"No. I don't have much money, and I need what little I've got to get back north."

Al pointed to the seat. "No charge, friend. For old time's sake. To celebrate you coming back. Sit down."

"No. I gotta leave. I just want to ask you something."

"All right, ask."

"I drove by your house a few minutes ago. I heard piano music."

He nodded. "You'll hear that a lot if you drive by our house."

"But this was ... somebody very ... talented."

Al smiled. "Andy Reed. Yeah, he's over most Saturday afternoons. He is very good. Been in competitions."

I must have frowned, because Al said, "Let me tell you some things, Luke. Let me bring you up to date. Have a seat there in Pete's chair. Don't leave just yet."

We both sat, and he said, "I know what you must be thinking. Why is that piano still there? You're wondering that. Right?

"That's what Doris and I asked ourselves, about six months after it happened. At first, of course, we couldn't do anything with it. Everything had to be left as it was—their rooms, their clothes, everything. Nothing moved, so that if they came back, everything would be just the way they left it. At that point we couldn't acknowledge that they would never come back. Mentally we could, but not deeper.

"But then after six months things changed. We couldn't stand to look at it. Every time we'd walk out the front door, we'd go right past it, and every time, it was like getting stabbed, ripped. In those days everything about this house, everything about this town, gave us the same feeling. We decided to leave. And I thought about you often in those days, Luke. I knew exactly why you did what you did. And I prayed that you were still alive ..."

He paused, and stared through the front window.

"Doris's brother in Dallas found a shop that needed a barber. We figured that would be far enough away. We could still come back and visit the graves.

"We didn't tell anybody until we put our house up for sale. That day we told people, and the real estate folks put the sign in our yard.

"About seven o'clock, after supper, we heard a knock. I went to the door, and there were maybe fifteen people standing on the front porch, mostly folks from the church, but a couple that I didn't know. Ben Halley was one of the people, and he said, 'Get Doris.'

"Doris came, and Ben said, 'We don't want you to leave.' Some of the people on the porch wept, and Doris wept.

"I told him we had to leave, we couldn't stand it, and he nodded. Then he said, 'The piano. We bought it, all of us. It belongs to the community, not to you.'

"I said, 'Yes. That's why we're gonna give it to the school.'

"Ben seemed ready for that. He shook his head. 'We bought it to go in this house, not in the school. Remember what you told us? You're the caretakers, you and Doris.'

"I lost my composure. I cursed him. I screamed at him, 'There's no one to play it! Go away!' No one moved.

"Then Dorothy Gaddis, the first teacher of all three of the girls, stepped out of that crowd and stood in front of the screen door, and Ben stepped back, and two other ladies that I didn't know stood beside Dorothy. She introduced the other two ladies as piano teachers, like her.

"She said, 'You have the finest piano in town. We want to come here and give all our lessons on your piano.' And the other two ladies nodded.

"I said, 'No. We're leaving.'

"Ben came forward again and said, 'Al and Doris, this town needs music so badly. And that music needs to come from this house, like it always has. Please stay, and let the teachers and the young people come into your home and make music.'

"Doris and I didn't say anything. We held each other and sobbed. After a few minutes the people all left the porch and walked away. I saw that the sign in our yard was gone.

"The next afternoon Dorothy Gaddis came over, and a little girl about eight was with her. 'We're here for the lesson,' Dorothy said, and Doris was gonna tell her no, but she looked at the girl and said all right. Well, when that little girl hit the first key, Doris almost had to run out of the house. She went to the bedroom and sobbed through the whole lesson.

"Dorothy taught two more children that day, and the next day one of the other teachers taught three students. And the pain didn't let up for Doris, but she didn't make 'em stop coming either.

"To make a long story short, we didn't leave. We decided to stay here in this town, where they love us, and when we die they can bury us next to the girls. Every day there's music in our house, and every day Doris bakes little sweets to give to the kids after their lessons. They love us. They invite us when they give recitals. We get special seats on the front row. It's still hard, very hard for us sometimes, but knowing they love us helps us make it.

"Some of those kids turn out to be very good pianists, Luke. You heard one of the best ones today, that Andy Reed. We remember when he started lessons, nine years ago. Now he's sixteen years old, and plays in competitions."

I stepped out of the chair and turned to him.

"When I heard that music today, I knew it was a good pianist, a trained pianist, but …"

Al frowned. "But what?"

I looked at the shelf behind Al's chair, and at the pictures on that shelf. "When you've heard a certain … sound come from that piano, you remember it."

Al rose from the chair and stared at me with wide eyes. "What do you mean?"

"I mean that boy was good, but …"

"But what?" His voice had changed, to a high, urgent pitch.

Something pulled the words right out of my mouth. "But …
there'll never be another Avis."

Al moaned, and his hands went to his face. He bent over and sat
in the customer chair under the window and sobbed. His body
shook.

I stared at him and said, "Oh, God, I'm sorry, Al, I didn't mean
to …"

Al shook his head, his face buried in his hands. He moaned and
sobbed.

"I'm so sorry, Al."

I turned to the door and put my hand on the knob. In my stu-
pidity I had hurt a good man. I needed to get in a boxcar and go far
away.

But Al stood and grabbed my shoulders. "No, no, no. You don't
understand. You don't understand. My soul needed to hear those
words. I never heard anything so beautiful. Luke, nobody ever
mentions the girls anymore. But you did. You remember. I never
heard anything so beautiful."

His expression changed, and his grip tightened. "Luke, you
have to go home with me right now. You have to say those words to
Doris. Come, let's go, now!"

He took my arm and pulled me out of the shop. "You drive. It'll
be quicker." A minute later we were on the front porch of the
house, and Al was yelling, "Doris! Doris!"

Al opened the screen and pulled me inside, and the boy at the
piano stopped playing and stared at us. Doris came out of the
kitchen, her eyes wide with fear. "What is it, Al?"

"Honey, it's Luke. Luke is here. Say the words, Luke. Now!"

I looked at Doris and said, "There'll never be another Avis."

Her mouth opened, and she ran to me and put her arms around
my neck. Her tears flowed onto my cheek. "Yes. There'll never be

another Avis. And there'll never be another Darla. And there'll never be another Annie. And there'll never be another *Marty*, Luke."

When she said *Marty*, I felt like someone had grabbed my insides and squeezed. For a second I couldn't get my breath.

I needed to be alone. I needed to think. I let go of Doris and said, "I've got to walk. I'll be back." I turned toward the door and opened the screen.

Al said, "Luke, your words came from God. Come back after your walk."

I stepped off the front porch and walked down the oil-top roads until I came to the tracks, the Overton-Henderson branch line. I headed east between the rails.

I think better when I'm walking. I figured I'd go down toward Henderson a ways and then come back.

I remembered walking those tracks as a boy, down by Overton. Must have been around six when I first did it. Walked on the rails, and kept my arms out straight for balance.

Six years old. 1919. Those were the good days. Lots of business at the sawmill. The farmers had money. Daddy came home happy when the mill was busy.

Things went bad a year later. The bottom dropped out for the farmers, and that hurt everybody. Daddy changed when his business went bad.

I remembered the late-night arguments in their bedroom. *You're drunk!* I heard her tell him. I didn't even know what that meant.

But I found out, about fifteen years later. Carol Tippitt. What a boozer.

I thought about Carol. I wondered what had happened to her. I thought about looking her up. Maybe I could take her back to Seattle with me. We could get drunk every night.

You're drunk. That's what Mom told Daddy. That's what Sis told me. So I was just like my Daddy.

At sundown I got to Henderson and turned around. My mind seemed fogged. I was replaying my whole life in my head, trying to get some clarity, to push the fog away. Tunes came into my head, Russ. The tunes from the hymns you sang. The words came too, words to go with the tunes. I tried to push those hymns out of my head. They wouldn't leave.

I started thinking about Vicky. So different from Carol and the others. Decent. Good-looking. But not even married. She told me she'd had offers. Why didn't she yes to one of them?

She helped me after it happened. Brought me food. Sat with me at the funeral. How did I thank her? One letter to say good-bye, then nothing. No contact. But she found me after I came back. Why? Why did she want to see me, after I'd been gone for ten years? But she did, even brought me a pie. Maybe she's not as smart as I thought.

Yeah, I guess I didn't treat her too well when she came to see me. But she didn't have to hit me in the face with that pie. What a waste.

I remembered Rie Erwin. Rie and Sis, always together, best friends, closer than sisters. Two, now one. Pretty Rie, wife and mother. I hurt her, but she forgave me. And she taught her little girl a prayer: *"God be with Luke."*

I'll never forget Rie standing by what was left of the school. Not so much as a bruise on her body. Others blown to bits, but her without a scratch. Why Rie? Why?

The woods, the tracks, had no answers for me. Night had fallen when I got back to New London, but I turned around in the darkness and went the other way. I had to keep walking. I still had those hymns going through my head. The words mixed with the voices from my past. Voices that said things like: *Why don't you know what Marty was wearing?*

I remembered the desert years. The dust, the dryness, so right for me. I belonged there. I thought, Maybe I'll go back. Maybe they're building another dam on the Columbia.

I wondered if Bob Coleman was up there somewhere. Nice fellow, but he worried too much about the river and the salmon. And he talked too much. I still remembered, *God has purposes.*

◆ ◆ ◆

I walked the tracks and talked out loud to the people from my past.

Purposes? Sure, Bob. Tell that to Al Fisher. He used to have three girls, Bob. Beautiful, all three!

Annie. Marty's friend. Latest shows, latest songs. Full of life, full of energy. She made that piano stand on end.

Darla. Middle child. Oh, she could pound out the ragtime. A boy named Paul liked her. He kissed her one day. But he'll never do it again. He got killed too.

Avis. The girl became a woman, and the woman's hands brought forth sounds so pretty they made me want to cry.

They made beautiful music, all three, and they got blown to pieces. So where's the purposes, Bob? Don't try to tell me about God, Mister!

But Al, I don't understand you either. Why is that piano still in the home, still making music? Why didn't you smash it with a sledgehammer, then burn it? You can't have things like that around, Al. They'll hurt you. I don't understand you, Al. Why are you still here? I'm sorry I mentioned Avis. I'm sorry I made you cry. Why did you tell me my words came from God? What kind of a God is that, who hurts you?

Russ, I talked to you out there on the tracks.

My baby sister liked to sing the hymns. She would have sung along with you, old man. She could have sung soprano to your baritone. You could have sung a duet. She would have liked you, Russ. She liked to talk, but she liked to be around quiet men. I wish you could have met her. She never knew her father. He died when she was two. You could have been like a grandfather to her.

I loved my sister, Russ. I thought she always knew that. But after Mom died, she thought she might be a burden to me. Then a judge asked me, "Do you want to take care of Marty?" And I said yes. Then Sis knew for sure that I loved her and wanted her. But he had to ask the question. I couldn't answer until he did.

Only the forest heard me. I got to Henderson again and turned around.

Daddy didn't want you, Sis. But I did. Oh, if I could take you to the tree cave just one more time. Come back, let's go there. Let me swing you out over the pond again.

Forgive me, Sis! I went to the school. Two days before! I knew there was a problem. I knew it was dangerous. I could have talked to a man about it. He might have done something. But I went out drinking instead. Judy brought an extra bottle, and we drank it. I was drunk the last time I looked at you. I was too drunk to even kiss you goodnight, before you went to heaven.

I started yelling into the forest, Russ. I stood between the rails and shouted. I tried to drown out the voices, and the songs. But I couldn't. The same words came back, over and over, all mixed together: *Why don't you know what Marty was wearing? ... I will arise and go to Jesus, He will embrace me in His arms ... I'm the*

luckiest girl that ever lived ... .and I still feel the same way ... Feelings lie buried that grace can restore ... You didn't kill her! Stop wallowing in it! ... Chords that are broken will vibrate once more ... God has purposes ... Jesus ready stands to save you, full of pity, love and power ... Nobody ever mentions the girls anymore. But you did. You remember ... There'll never be another Avis ... Your words came from God ... You're drunk ... There's a wideness in God's mercy ... .

I stood and screamed into the forest. I had been out there all night. The eastern sky was turning gray.

Then something happened. And for three weeks I've been trying to think of a way to explain it to you.

Remember when I told you about Bob Coleman finding my ledge on the canyon wall? Remember that little conversation we had one Sunday, sitting on that ledge? Coleman asked me if I thought the dam could stop the river. He said that when he was down close and saw the river's power, he wasn't sure a dam could stop it.

Well, there was a dam inside me. All the guilt and grief and bitterness had built up a dam, high and thick like Grand Coulee. In front of that dam was a dry and barren valley. But behind the dam was the river.

You put a crack in that dam, Russ. I don't understand how you did it. You hardly ever talked to me. I don't think you even listened to me half the time. But you fed me, and gave me a place to sleep, and you gave my hands work. And you sang your songs.

The waters found the crack and pushed into it. The dam held for a while, but Al Fisher's words widened the crack.

I stood on the tracks, shouting into the forest in the dark. I cursed. I shouted the word "Christ!" I said the word again, softly.

The dam split open. Broke apart, and gave way to the waters.

The waters crumbled the concrete and boiled into the valley with a mighty surge and roar like rolling thunder. The white water carried the dam away, all the concrete and hardness, every bit. It all happened in one second. And then a river flowed in the valley, deep and wide, like the old Columbia.

I began to cry for Sis. I had never done that before, not in ten years since it happened. What a glory to cry for her! I wept for two hours while the sun rose. The river didn't take away my sorrow. My sorrow became part of the river, and I knew it would be there always, even after I'm gone.

I went back to Al and Doris. They were just sitting down to breakfast. Told me they'd been worried. I tried to explain what had happened, that I'd been in the dark for ten years, like inside the tunnel, but the sun had come up that morning. They seemed to understand. I asked Al to give me a haircut and a shave, and told them I wanted to go to church. He said he had never cut hair on a Sunday before, but he did it, right after breakfast.

I went back to your house and put on the brown suit you left. I drove to the church. Al and Doris were already there, in the choir. I walked in as they were singing the opening hymn. I looked to the left, near the front, and saw her just where she said she'd be. *Creature of habit.* I went up and moved into the pew next to her.

When Vicky saw me, her hymnal fell to the floor. She picked it up and turned to the page. I helped her hold the book.

You know what song it was, Russ? "Christ, Whose Glory Fills the Skies." I think Vicky was too shocked to sing. But I sang. I sang those words, and wished I had a voice like yours, old man.

32

Russ

*I*t is March of 1948. Winter lingers, and sends cold winds from the north to irritate us, to remind us he'll be back. But his victories are short-lived. The sun lifts into the sky with ease and stays longer each day. Fat robins land in my back yard hoping for a meal from the garden dirt. Early bluebonnets and Indian paintbrushes dot the roadsides, and the sycamores and elms are bursting with new green.

I need to put down this pen and pick up a hoe. Spring means turning the earth and planting, and feeling the good sun on face and arms. It's time to bring this story to a close and get outdoors. But there's a bit more to tell.

◆ ◆ ◆

It was early October, a couple of weeks after I'd returned from Dallas. I took my truck into Overton for some brake work. Luke was still working with Dewey at that time, and he told me they were pretty busy that morning, and he wouldn't be able to get to my truck for a few hours. So he drove me back home in Dewey's truck.

I fixed and ate dinner, then went to the bedroom and took off my shoes for a nap, my usual routine on days I don't have outdoor work. I woke up to a noise from my kitchen.

I stepped into the hall and heard a gasp from the red-haired woman standing next to the kitchen table, holding a dish wrapped in tinfoil.

We stared at each other. She said, "I didn't know you were here."

I smiled. "Mrs. Halley, I'm so happy to be able to thank you for bringing the pies and cakes and chicken all these years. I've enjoyed those dishes so much."

She frowned and said softly, "You've known it was me?"

I nodded. "I saw your car in the country lane five years ago. I never mentioned it because I knew you wanted the secrecy. But now that you're here, I need to ask you, why are you so good to me?"

She looked away.

I said, "Would you stay for a while and have coffee with me?" I pulled out a chair, and she put down the dish and sat. A few minutes later I poured us both a cup and sat facing her.

She said, "This is going to be hard for me to do, but I should tell you. You need to know."

She took a sip of coffee. "Tim died. My son. My only child. You were in the pulpit. You were supposed to preach his funeral."

My heart jumped a beat.

"You never looked at us. You didn't say a word."

I swallowed and breathed very deeply.

"I sat on the pew, waiting to hear your words. But you were silent, Mr. Smith. You left the pulpit without saying anything.

"So many died. And they each got a funeral on Saturday. Fifteen minutes. In and out. All the same. Same hymns. Same Bible verses. But Tim's funeral was different."

I sat there slack-jawed. I wanted to speak, but nothing seemed right.

"In those first days my shock and grief kept me from thinking about that funeral with no words. A few months later I entered into a deep depression over the loss of my son. I wanted to take my own life. I came very close to doing that. The night was so black, like in a deep cave.

"But one star shone in that black night. You were that star. You gave my son a special funeral. You just stood in that pulpit and prayed for a few minutes, then left. That memory, that star, saved me. I decided to live.

"I didn't see you again until two years later, when you joined the church. I still remember my shock when you stood in front and turned to face the congregation. It's him, I told myself. Why has he come back?"

I had to interrupt her. "Ma'am, I need to tell you the truth about why I didn't say anything that morning."

"Oh, I know. You had a stroke. You couldn't speak words."

My world came to a stop. I just stared at her, with wide eyes and an open mouth.

"But you prayed up there. Oh, I can tell when a man's really praying. You wanted so much to preach, to comfort us. But words wouldn't have meant a thing. I would have forgotten them. Seeing you pray, though, is something I won't ever forget.

"You're wondering how I know about the stroke. After you joined our church, I had to find out why you came back. I asked some folks who had come to the funeral, who was the man who didn't speak? I finally learned you were Pastor Smith from Nacogdoches. I drove to Nacogdoches. I found the church where you used to preach. I talked to people. You know what they said? They said you had lost your mind when you went to preach a funeral after the explosion. That was real easy to believe back then. What happened was so horrible, so unthinkable, that people could readily believe that even a preacher, who had been around death plenty of times, might lose his mind when confronted by such horror. The people told me about you being at Rusk Hospital, and said that they didn't know what had happened to you since then. Assumed you'd gone to live with your daughter or one of your sons in Dallas.

"I was determined to learn the truth. From the Nacogdoches folks I finally got an address for your daughter in Dallas. I went to visit her. Told her I visited your former congregation and that I wanted to know how you were doing. In the course of the conversation your daughter mentioned the misdiagnosis and the real reason you were sent to Rusk.

"I followed you home from church one day. That's how I learned where you live. I heard you did gardening work around town. I thought about hiring you to put in a garden for me, so I could talk to you and learn why you came back. I decided against doing that. You wanted your past to be a secret, for whatever reason.

"But I wanted to let you know that somebody cared about you. So I brought the food."

My heartbeat slowed and a great peace settled over me. I said, "I want you to keep bringing the food. But you can come to the front door now."

She shook her head. "No."

"But why not? We both know—"

"You and I have no secrets. But other people might get the wrong idea if they saw me visit you."

"What idea? What's wrong with a lady bringing a pie to an old man?"

Her face turned a shade of pink, and I saw the tiniest trace of a smile. In a voice as soft as a snowflake she said, "But I'm a married woman, and … you're a handsome man."

Her words seemed to bounce in my head before coming to rest. I just stared at her. She finally reached over, patted my hand, and said, "I'll be back for my bowl in a month." She rose, stepped out my back door, and walked past the garden to the country lane and her car.

◆ ◆ ◆

I told Luke about Sue's visit on the way back to Overton to get my truck.

He said, "You know what your problem is, Russ? You like your secrets. You let secrets play a big role in your life. Too big. For years you didn't tell Sue you knew she brought the food. You should have. You could have made a friend. Sue's probably lonely, she would have enjoyed your friendship. But you let the secret rule.

"And your other secret, about the mental hospital. You don't need it. The Nacogdoches folks were scared of you because you had changed from the Gabby they knew. But around here, the people never knew Gabby. They know *you*. Russ, the quiet man, the gardener and landscaper. Nobody cares about your past. You're part of the community. Think about it."

I did think about it, over the next few days. And I thought about Luke. What happened in the past had ruled him, kept him chained, for ten years, but the day came when those chains broke, and now he's free.

I decided Luke was right. My past didn't need to rule me either. I gave up that secret. I didn't go around telling everyone about my previous life, but neither did I try to hide it. And so far I've never needed to.

◆ ◆ ◆

Luke worked in Dewey's garage for a couple of months, but finally landed a job in the oil field, maintaining and repairing the engines like he did in the past. He found a room in Kilgore and moved out of my house.

One Sunday right before Christmas I heard a knock, and when I opened the door Vicky and Luke were there, standing real close to each other. I invited them in, and we all sat. I offered to make coffee, but they shook their heads. Then they looked at each other, and Vicky turned to me and said, "We want you to marry us."

It took me a second or two to swallow that, but then I shook my head. "You need a preacher."

She said, "We've cleared it with the preacher. You can do it. You're ordained."

I shook my head again. "So Luke told you about me. That's okay. But I'm not that man anymore."

Her soft smile seemed to fill the room. "I don't want Gabby to marry us. I want you to marry us. I know you're not the man you were. Neither is Luke, and you're a big reason why. You brought him back."

"Oh, no. Wasn't me."

"You know what I mean, Russ."

"And you know what *I* mean, Vicky."

She nodded, grinned, and gave me a wink, and her face radiated a joy I could almost reach out and touch. I said, "I'll do it on one condition."

"What's your condition, preacher man?"

"Vicky, Luke told me a story. And the story had an ending. He walked into a church on a Sunday morning and stood next to you and sang with you. But …"

She grinned. "But what?"

"But he ended the story a little too soon. Now, call me a nosy old man. Call me a snoop, a busybody. I don't want to know all about your courtship. I just want to know one thing. Tell me that, and I'll agree to marry you."

"What, Russ?"

"What did you say to each other when you walked out of the church that morning?"

They looked at each other and burst into laughter. I realized I had never before seen Luke Robertson laugh. It felt good to see that.

They calmed down, and Luke spoke first. "We didn't say anything at first. We just walked out of the sanctuary with the others and went a little ways away from the church. Then Vicky turned to me and said, 'Why did you shave?'"

Vicky said, "And Luke's reply was, 'I never could get all the pie out of my beard. Had to cut it off.'"

The laughter of love filled the room.

So, early in the new year I stood below the pulpit where I once couldn't speak and read them their vows. What an occasion. Rie Lacefield came all the way from California, and I got to witness that glorious reunion before the ceremony. Al and Doris Fisher came, and Tom and Rachel Erwin, Ben and Sue Halley, Dewey, and even cousin Kelly. An unforgettable day. But that was just the beginning. Last month Luke and Vicky made me promise to baptize the baby they're expecting in October. It is a great joy for an old man to have young friends.

So I guess I'm still a preacher, of sorts. And I do think about Gabby often, and about the woman who loved him. Gabby *was* a good man. He did help and comfort people. He spoke with great talent, but he didn't realize the power of words, and wasted them.

Gabby would have been excited to hear the last part of Luke's story. He would have loved to interpret, to explain, to analyze, to generalize what happened to Luke out on the railroad tracks.

What a great sermon that man could have preached. Or so *he* would have thought.

I joined the church choir a month ago. The director lady doesn't always pick the songs I would pick, but I sing anyway. It does seem right to be singing with others rather than alone. The cicadas have always known that.

I've been to some church socials, and look forward to the spring and summer picnics. But I won't be here all summer. I've got plans for a long trip. I'm going to get on a train and ride to Portland, Oregon.

You see, one part of Luke's story has always bothered me. He and Bob Coleman were down by the river, and Coleman asked Luke a question. Luke cursed Coleman and walked away. They never saw each other again. So Coleman's last memory of Luke is a memory of a curse.

That's not right. A curse is like a blessing—its words have a power, and linger in the heart. Deep inside I feel that Coleman remembers Luke and his curse.

I plan to find Bob Coleman. I will take this story to him and let him read it, so he'll understand why Luke cursed him. And when he reads the end of the story, he'll know that Luke is not hardened and bitter any longer but is a new man, made right, made whole by a power only Luke himself can describe. I feel that when Coleman realizes what happened, he'll forget the curse and share Luke's joy.

It might take me a while to track him down. I might have to go up into Washington, and follow the big river through the Cascades into the desert. Wouldn't surprise me if they're building another dam out there somewhere. Seems like men just can't help building dams.

I want to see the rivers Luke talked about, both of them. With his eyes he saw the Columbia, surging clear and cold through the scrub desert toward the Pacific. The other river he saw with his soul.

You might think I'd have already seen that second river. It flowed close, almost in Gabby's back yard, but he was too busy talking to really notice it. As for me, the fears and secrets kept me in a fog, so I didn't see the river either, not in its glory, not the way Luke saw it. I feel a great need to see it, the way he saw it, before I leave.

Bob Coleman's up there somewhere. I'll find him. But for now I'll close with words he said to Luke on a ledge above the mighty Columbia: There is a depth and a great power to the water. And a wideness.

Well, that last word was mine. Time to pick up that hoe.

THERE IS A
WIDENESS

Branching Out

*A guide for personal reflection
or group discussion*

When you pass through the waters, I will be with you; and when you pass through the rivers, they will not sweep over you.

—*Isaiah 43:2*

Branching Out

Tragedy strikes each of us in various ways. When it hits, our lives are thrown off course—or are they? Is it possible there is a reason we have to walk through horrible events? Use the following questions, and others you come up with, to walk with Russ and Luke and see where their paths take them.

Many contemporary novels have female protagonists and feminine viewpoints. Why do you think the author chose men as his main characters? Could a similar story be told with female main characters? In what ways would the story necessarily be different with female main characters?

One of the themes of the story is forgiveness. Why does Avis tell her father to forgive her "because I asked you?" Yet Rie forgives Luke for disappearing from her life even though he does not ask for her forgiveness. Discuss the difference. Who does Luke need to forgive?

The well blowout foreshadows the school tragedy. What other events and comments in the first half of the story foreshadow the tragedy?

When they first meet, who needs redemption more, Luke or Russ?

During their time together, Russ never talks much to Luke, yet Russ influences Luke profoundly. Why? What exactly does Russ do for Luke?

Avis tells her father that she "needs fixing." Why? Do you "need fixing?"

Historically, a Court of Inquiry that was convened soon after the school explosion concluded that no individual was personally responsible and that prosecution was not warranted. What do you think? What would be the reaction to a tragedy with similar loss of life today?

Russ says that Gabby could "talk without thinking." Can words uttered with no thought behind them still comfort a listener? Do you know people who "talk without thinking?"

Discuss the significance of dawns in the story.

What adjective, used by one of Luke's dates to describe him, might help explain his reaction to the tragedy?

Vicky turns down marriage proposals from good men. Why? Is she waiting for Luke to return? Is that rational? Has he ever shown interest in her? Is she letting her heart lead her head?

What drew Russ back to the very church where he failed to preach a funeral?

Was Al Fisher's loss in the explosion greater than Luke's? Why did Luke leave and why did Al stay?

Russ regains his use of words by singing. Is a song more than words put to music? Can anything be more than the sum of its parts?

Can Luke's night on the railroad tracks, after his visit to Al Fisher, be considered one long prayer, a need in search of a word? Can a person who rejects God pray? Does God hear the prayer of one who rejects Him?

Luke's life-changing enlightenment occurs in a dramatic single moment, which he describes in terms of a dam breaking. Are "conversions" necessary for persons to feel redeemed? Can one "see the river" without a life-changing experience?

Vicky tells Luke to "stop wallowing in it." In our modern age of tragedies, do you feel that we "wallow" in them excessively? Give examples.

Luke and Vicky finally marry in their mid-thirties. How well do you think they know each other? Are they a good match?

In what significant way is Luke like his father?

Why does Russ feel a need to share Luke's story?

Several rivers are mentioned in the Bible. Which one most closely resembles the river that Luke, according to Russ, "saw with his soul?" Identify chapters and verses.

The Word at Work . . .

*W*hat would you do if you wanted to share God's love with children on the streets of your city? That's the dilemma David C. Cook faced in 1870s Chicago. His answer was to create literature that would capture children's hearts.

Out of those humble beginnings grew a worldwide ministry that has used literature to proclaim God's love and disciple generation after generation. Cook Communications Ministries is committed to personal discipleship—to helping people of all ages learn God's Word, embrace his salvation, walk in his ways, and minister in his name.

Opportunities—and Crisis

We live in a land of plenty—including plenty of Christian literature! But what about the rest of the world? Jesus commanded, "Go and make disciples of all nations" (Matt. 28:19) and we want to obey this commandment. But how does a publishing organization "go" into all the world?

There are five times as many Christians around the world as there are in North America. Christian workers in many of these countries have no more than a New Testament, or perhaps a single shared copy of the Bible, from which to learn and teach.

We are committed to sharing what God has given us with such Christians.

A vital part of Cook Communications Ministries is our international out-reach, Cook Communications Ministries International (CCMI). Your purchase of this book, and of other books and Christian-growth products from Cook, enables CCMI to provide Bibles and Christian literature to people in more than 150 languages in 65 countries.

Cook Communications Ministries is a not-for-profit, self-supporting organization. Revenues from sales of our books, Bible curriculum, and other church and home products not only fund our U.S. ministry, but also fund our CCMI ministry around the world. One hundred percent of donations to CCMI go to our international literature programs.

. . . Around the World

CCMI reaches out internationally in three ways:

· Our premier International Christian Publishing Institute (ICPI) trains leaders
from nationally led publishing houses around the world to develop evangelism
and discipleship materials to transform lives in their countries.

· We provide literature for pastors, evangelists, and Christian workers in their
national language. We provide study helps for pastors and lay leaders in many
parts of the world, such as China, India, Cuba, Iran, and Vietnam.

· We reach people at risk—refugees, AIDS victims, street children, and famine
victims—with God's Word. CCMI puts literature that shares the Good News
into the hands of people at spiritual risk—people who might die before they
hear the name of Jesus and are transformed by his love.

Word Power—God's Power

Faith Kidz, RiverOak, Honor, Life Journey, Victor, NexGen — every time you purchase a book produced by Cook Communications Ministries, you not only meet a
vital personal need in your life or in the life of someone you love, but you're also
a part of ministering to José in Colombia, Humberto in Chile, Gousa in India, or
Lidiane in Brazil. You help make it possible for a pastor in China, a child in Peru,
or a mother in West Africa to enjoy a life-changing book. And because you
helped, children and adults around the world are learning God's Word and walking in his ways.

Thank you for your partnership in helping to disciple the world. May God
bless you with the power of his Word in your life.

*For more information about our
international ministries, visit
www.ccmi.org.*